The Northport Coffee Group

José F. Nodar

Camden Books Publishing

The Northport Coffee Group / José F. Nodar
ISBN 978-1-7643409-0-8 - Paperback
ISBN 978-1-7643409-1-5 - E-pub

Dedication

In loving memory of my wife,
Miriam Vassallo Nodar,
and her enduring presence.
You are always in my thoughts.
For anyone who's ever loved deeply, lost fully, and still found
the courage to begin again.

Table of Contents

CHAPTER 1

The Northport Coffee Group

Nestled between low, rolling hills and framed by sunburnt paddocks and gumtree-lined back roads, Northport, New South Wales, is the kind of place where everyone knows everyone—or at least their cousin.

We're about eighty kilometres south of Sydney, just far enough to stay out of its shadow but close enough to catch its glow. And by 2025, somehow, Northport had managed to hang onto its old charm, despite the spread of suburbia slowly creeping toward us like rising floodwater.

At the heart of town is our modest but bustling main street: wide, with some angled parking, faded pedestrian crossings, and shops housed in a mix of old brick and fibro, many with verandahs shading the cracked footpaths. The signs on most businesses have been sun-faded into near illegibility, but nobody seems to mind.

There's Tucker's General Store, the place that stocks everything from bread and milk to tractor oil and fishing lures. It still survives, even thrives, despite the two supermarket giants, Coles, and Woolworths, planted like unwelcome siblings at the edge of town. Next door is Joanne's and Mick's Hair & Beauty, a two-chair salon that doubles as Northport's unofficial information hub. Gossip gets trimmed and blow-dried there faster than anywhere else.

Across the street stands the Australia Post office, which also sells lottery tickets and greeting cards-birthdays, condolences, and the occasional cheeky anniversary card. A few doors down is the Northport Café & Bakery, where you'll find the best pies, sausage rolls, and caramel slices this side of the Hume, served with a smile and, more often than not, a chat about someone's cousin's gallbladder surgery.

Bill's Mitre 10 Hardware, The Village Book & Stuff (which sells both rare books and just-right birthday pens), and Northport Rural Supplies keep the town ticking, especially for the folks still on the land. At the corner, there's the Northport Medical Practice, where Dr William Ellis, our long-time GP, sees patients Monday to Thursday. Beside it is Smith & Sons Butchery, now owned by Charlie Ng, who kept the original name either out of nostalgia or thrift. Charlie still wraps meat in brown paper, which makes everything feel fresher and more proper somehow.

And then there's the Northport Tavern, with its creaky stools, salty Schnitzels, decent beer, and the only place in town to yell at the footy without judgment.

Northport spans only about a dozen streets.

You'll find weatherboard homes, fibro cottages, and the occasional flashy brick veneer-the hallmark of someone who's "done well" and knocked down their parents' house to build something with a remote-controlled garage. Lawns are mostly tidy, if dry.

Dogs bark behind low fences.

Mailboxes are hand-painted or repurposed from milk cans, gumboots, or rusting toolboxes.

Bicycles lie on verges.

Scooters abandon themselves in driveways.

Cricket stumps lean against trees like forgotten ambitions.

Evenings in Northport are a ritual.

People gather near their porches or out by the carport with a cold one in hand, watching the sun disappear behind the hills while magpies sing and cockatoos squawk their disdain. On Saturdays, the whirr of lawnmowers is the soundtrack of suburban pride.

We've got both a primary and a high school, tucked on the eastern side of town, separated by a dusty soccer oval and a patch of bush. Northport Primary is a cheerful sprawl of older brick buildings painted with student murals, some of them decades old.

The high school's a bit more serious, with about two hundred kids and a teaching staff who double as coaches, counsellors, and, on trivia night, fierce competitors. Both schools share a hall that hosts assemblies, talent shows, the occasional funeral, and the yearly bush dance, where everyone forgets the two-step and just stomps with joy.

Our hospital is small but mighty: six wards, a 24-hour emergency room, and a crew of nurses and doctors who mostly live within shouting distance. If you break a wrist or have a baby, you're in excellent hands. Anything trickier, you'll be heading up the highway.

By 2025, life in Northport wasn't always easy.

The drought years were hard, but they were stitched together with community cuppas, neighbourly favours, and secrets quietly passed behind hedges or over shop counters.

And then one morning, a notice appeared on the community board outside Tucker's General Store that changed everything-at least for me, and eventually for a few others too.

Seeking Ladies for Coffee, Conversation, and Possibly Mischief.

Retired academic, new to town, invites like-minded women to form a monthly social group.

Interests: books, stories, secrets, and shared laughter.

First meeting at Northport Café & Bakery – Saturday, 10 a.m.

Signed,
Eleanor Whitman

That was me.

And no, I didn't expect much from it either.

I'd moved to Northport six months earlier, after Charles, my husband of forty years, had passed away quietly, painfully, and far too soon. We'd lived most of our lives in Sydney. I taught literature and feminist theory at the University of Sydney and, under a pen name that not even Charles fully approved of, I wrote steamy, unapologetically saucy novels.

After he was gone, our big old townhouse felt more like a mausoleum than a home.

The silence rang too loud.

CHAPTER 2

Caffeine and Secrets

The café bakery was already warm with the scent of fresh scones and the wonderfully just-ground coffee beans when I pushed two tables aside and arranged a loose circle of mismatched chairs near the back corner, beneath the faded mural of the Nepean River. The mural had been there for years.

Sunlight had drained most of the blue from the water, and the gumtrees looked ghostly, but I liked the quiet backdrop. It felt like the right place for something to begin.

Outside, the breeze rustled the trees gently. Inside, though, the air buzzed with a different kind of energy-curiosity, maybe.

Or anticipation.

A quiet tension, waiting to be named.

One by one, they came.

And none of them came empty-handed.

Fiona Grant was first.

Tall, crisp, no-nonsense. She wore navy slacks and a silk blouse that looked like it belonged in a courtroom-or had taken down a few in its time. She gave me a firm handshake and did a sweep of the room like she was assessing potential threats. I smiled anyway.

She didn't show the strain-none of them did, at first.

But I'd learn soon enough that Fiona was holding her life together with hope, habit, and minimum payments on credit cards she had told no one about. There were late-night poker tabs bookmarked on her laptop and unopened envelopes stacked on her kitchen table. Her perfectly tailored life was teetering on the edge of unravelling.

Next was Natalie Cho, thirty-eight, and as quiet as a whisper. She slipped in almost unnoticed, clutching a worn sketchbook to her chest as if it could deflect questions. She wore a cardigan despite the warmth and offered a small smile when I greeted her. When someone asked about her week, her eyes darted like a deer in tall grass.

Natalie's art was luminous, magical even. But no brushstroke could paint over the whispers that followed her around town.

Her husband had vanished a year ago.

No note.

No trace.

Just silence, an open front door, and a house that echoed with uncertainty.

The police hadn't closed the case. And Natalie had told no one the entire story, including what had happened that night.

Then came Shanice Reed, twenty-nine, all sunglasses, sass, and a dress that could start a conversation in any city. She breezed in like a summer storm, loud and glittering. She'd just landed a major boutique deal in Sydney, she said so with a bright smile that didn't quite reach her eyes.

She kept glancing at her phone. I could guess why. Pregnant, and unsure who the father was-either a Brisbane creative director or the bartender from her last launch party.

She hadn't told her mother.

She hadn't told anyone.

And the clock was ticking louder each day.

Bethany Clark arrived with a small tray of her lemon slices "just like Mum used to make," and before she'd even sat down, I heard someone whisper, "Isn't she lovely?"

She was.

Sixty, kind-eyed, and wearing a floral blouse that matched the Tupperware lid. She was everyone's nan within minutes.

But there was a flicker in Bethany's gaze, like something long dormant still glowed. She'd once gone by another name, decades ago-a name whispered in connection with a radical group, a mysterious bombing, and a chapter of history most had forgotten. Most, but not all.

Zoe Chen swept in late, all city polish and designer sharpness. Her phone buzzed relentlessly in her handbag as she offered a breathless apology. A blazer over a fitted dress, a wedding ring, and a daughter back home. She split her weeks between Sydney and Northport, trying to keep everything in balance. Or appearing to.

What she hadn't told anyone-not even herself, maybe-was that she'd found something. A hotel receipt. A gap on the calendar. And then the sudden, awful possibility: her husband had another family. Somewhere else. She hadn't decided what to do. But her daughter was asking questions now.

Naomi Jackson came in next, in scrubs splattered with coffee and with a grin that could slice through stone. She was forty-five, worked at the hospital, and made everyone laugh within five minutes. "The only man I can tolerate is my spaniel," she said, and they loved her for it.

But I saw the fatigue behind the humour.

I always do.

Three years ago, she'd made a call that might have cost a young boy his life. She carried that weight quietly and had been sending anonymous money to the family ever since, hoping guilt could be softened by good intentions.

Then came Bea, Beatrice Torrance, thirty-four, but insisted on "Bea."

She lit up the room with her laughter, her movement, her breathwork talk, and her firm belief in lavender oil. She radiated energy. But energy can be armour, too.

Bea was in love.

With her best friend's husband.

And she suspected the feeling was mutual.

The guilt wrapped around her like ivy-slow and choking. No amount of chakra cleansing was going to make that ache disappear.

Di arrived shortly after-Diana Williams, but she went by Di.

CHAPTER 3

Truth, Honesty, Coffee and Wine

It was two weeks later when the women found themselves gathered, not in the hum of the Northport Café, but in Eleanor Whitman's cosy, book-filled cottage on Jacaranda Street.

Eleanor had pushed the furniture aside to make space for a loose circle of armchairs, mismatched cushions, and the odd beanbag for the more adventurous (or younger) members. The scent of freshly brewed coffee filled the air, mingling with something rich and earthy from the kitchen, a slow-cooked beef stew Eleanor had thrown together earlier.

On a side table sat a carafe of red wine, a platter of cheeses and crackers, and a pot of strong black coffee, already half-empty.

They chatted easily at first about work, children, weather, and the disastrous state of the Northport High School toilets until Eleanor clapped her hands once, lightly.

"All right," she said, smiling warmly, but with that undeniable twinkle of authority in her eye. "Since this is our first official meeting of the Northport Coffee Group, I thought it best we establish a few gentle guidelines."

The women leaned forward, some playful, some wary.

"Nothing formal, nothing frightening," Eleanor continued. "Simply three things I propose we agree upon: truth, honesty, and coffee." She paused, tilting her head, then added, "And, optionally, wine."

The room rippled with soft laughter.

"Truth and honesty?" Bea grinned, swirling her wine. "Aren't those the same thing?"

Eleanor shook her head thoughtfully. "Truth is what you know in your bones. Honesty is what you're willing to admit out loud."

A silence fell, comfortable for some, prickling for others.

Naomi Jackson leaned back in her chair, arms folded. "Sounds dangerous," she said, a teasing glint in her eye. "I'm in."

"I like the wine part," Shanice piped up, raising her glass. "Makes the first two a lot easier."

Natalie Cho hugged a cushion to her chest but nodded slightly, her dark hair falling across her face. Diana Williams offered a small, guarded smile. George gave a theatrical shrug.

"Bring on the truth," she said, "as long as nobody expects me to confess my undying love for instant coffee."

Laughter again, but underneath it, something like relief.

As if they all recognised, maybe for the first time in a long time, that this was a place they might not have to pretend.

Eleanor leaned forward, her silver curls bouncing softly. "One more thing," she said. "For our next meeting, two weeks from now, I'd like each of you to bring your favourite mug, yes, your real favourite-and a story. It can be funny, painful, ridiculous, profound. Anything you wish. But it must be real."

There were some murmurs and raised eyebrows.

"My favourite mug is chipped and ugly," Zoe admitted, a little sheepishly.

"Perfect," Eleanor said with a warm smile. "Scars make things more beautiful."

Vivian watched her carefully from across the circle, studying every word, every gesture.

Fiona Grant, arms crossed, considered for a long moment. "Fine," she said finally. "But don't expect a Disney ending."

"Never," Eleanor promised. "Only truth, only honesty, with a side of caffeine and fermented grapes."

And so, it was agreed, and Zoe 'volunteered' to go first with her story, and she received a big round of applause for her effort.

As the evening wore on and the wine flowed more freely, the conversations loosened, stories slipped out like small birds finally uncaged. Nothing too heavy yet, just glimpses: Naomi talking about her wild sons, Shanice recounting a disastrous fashion show in Byron Bay, George describing a camel race she once stumbled into in Morocco.

But underneath the laughter, there was a growing sense that something was beginning here, something none of them could quite name yet.

When the last of the women had gone, leaving behind a trail of empty wineglasses and half-hearted promises to help clean up next time, Eleanor stood alone in the centre of her living room. The hum of voices and laughter still clung to the walls, a ghost of the gathering.

She exhaled, a soft, satisfied breath. The first meeting had gone better than she dared hope.

Eleanor tidied methodically, her body moving on autopilot: stacking plates, wiping wine rings from the coffee table, folding the worn plaid throw draped over the arm of a chair. These small acts of order anchored her.

When the last mug was rinsed and placed on the drying rack, she allowed herself a moment of stillness.

The house, once filled with the comfortable clutter of a shared life, had grown quieter since Roger's passing.

Sometimes too quiet. And though she had always loved solitude, lately it had started to ache around the edges.

She climbed the narrow staircase, her fingers brushing the polished wood of the banister, and stopped before a simple white door at the end of the hall.

Her secret room.

Roger had suggested that she should have her space once she'd first started dabbling seriously in fiction. "Every queen needs her castle," he'd said. After his passing and Eleanor's move to Northport, that was exactly what she created.

Inside, the walls were lined with bookshelves sagging under the weight of old paperbacks, reference books, and journals. A battered oak desk sat under the slanted window, overlooking the jacarandas that dusted the street below in purple petals.

CHAPTER 4

Zoe's Balancing Act

Two weeks later, my living room came to life again. The women returned, each one carrying a mug, tucked under their arms, peeking out of tote bags, or clutched proudly in their hands like holy relics from some sacred temple of caffeine. It was beautiful, in that quiet, unexpected way life sometimes is.

Naomi held up hers first, a blindingly bright pink thing with "#MumLife – Powered by Caffeine and Chaos" stamped across it in chaotic lettering.

"Oh my God, Naomi, what is that?" Bea burst out laughing, nearly dropping her own.

Naomi grinned wickedly. "It's not a mug. It's a cry for help."

Laughter erupted around the room.

It was infectious.

Warm.

The kind of sound that fills up a space and your chest all at once.

Just what we all needed.

Vivian, more reserved, had brought a lovely handmade ceramic piece. Soft eucalyptus leaves circled the outside in delicate brushstrokes. She held it as if it might shatter. "Found it at the op-shop," she murmured. "It felt calm."

Fiona's mug was exactly what I expected:

Sleek, black, and emblazoned in bold white lettering: Do I Look Like I Have Time for Your Nonsense?

"It keeps people from bothering me in the office," she said flatly. Another burst of laughter followed.

Bethany arrived with something you'd expect to see in a BBC period drama: a fine floral china, dainty, with a gold rim and matching saucer. Diana's, as always, matched her: matte navy, clean, minimalist, professional. George had a mug with a cartoon koala in full lotus pose. "I like balance," she quipped with a wink.

"Okay, okay, show and tell is over!" Shanice declared with dramatic flair. "Now, can someone please pour the wine?"

I uncorked the bottle, passing it around as the voices rose. Laughter tumbled from every corner. It was chaotic and glorious. This gathering of souls that once thought they were strangers.

After a while, I raised my hand, just slightly, an old habit from lecturing.

The room stilled almost immediately, that silent hush of attention I always found so reverent.

"Ladies," I began, looking at each of them, "thank you for bringing your beautiful mugs. Each one tells a story." I let that sit for a moment. "And speaking of stories, Zoe, you were brave enough to volunteer last time. Are you ready?"

Zoe, seated beside the armchair, gave a small nod.

She set down her pristine white mug, a minimalist design with a single red stripe, and straightened her blazer, despite the fact we weren't in court or at a board meeting. Her fingers trembled before she folded them carefully into her lap.

"I've thought a lot about this evening," she said.

Her voice was steady, but soft.

"And I've realised I don't have anyone to talk to. Not really. Not about the big stuff. But somehow, even though we only met a few weeks ago, this space you've created, Eleanor, this space we've created, feels safe. So, I'm going to speak freely. And maybe you'll have suggestions. Or at least understanding."

All around the room, I watched heads nod gently.

Zoe took a breath. "I'm used to control," she said. "Structure. I'm a corporate lawyer. I live by schedules, clauses, clear terms. Problems I can solve. But life doesn't always respect rules."

She paused.

I could see her pushing back tears.

She wouldn't let them fall.

Not yet.

"I met my husband, Ethan, when I was twenty-three. He was older. Calm. Brilliant. The first person to believe I belonged in law. And for years, he's been... my person. Or I thought he was."

The room collectively inhaled, but no one said a word.

Zoe pressed on. "Lately, things have felt off. Subtle shifts. He travels more. He asks fewer questions. He listens less. And then three weeks ago, I found a receipt in the pocket of his coat. From a jewellery store in Sydney."

"Was it for you?" Natalie asked gently.

Zoe shook her head. "No. Not my size. Not my style. There's been no occasion. He hasn't given me anything in, well, a long time."

The room held its breath.

"Could it be for someone else?" Bethany asked softly.

"Maybe. Probably." Zoe exhaled.

"When I asked him about it, he lied. Said it was for a colleague's retirement. But I checked. That colleague retired last year."

"Classic misdirection," Fiona muttered into her wine.

"Men," Naomi sighed. "It's always jewellery or perfume. Never a receipt from Bunnings. That's when you know they're innocent."

The laughter was swift, welcome, a valve of release. Even Zoe chuckled, though hers ended abruptly, the weight still pressing.

"I haven't confronted him again," she said.

"I don't know how. Or what to believe. I'm scared. Of what I'll find. Of what it'll do to our daughter. And to whatever's left of our marriage."

There was a pause.

Then, Vivian reached across and gently touched Zoe's hand. "Maybe it's not what you think," she offered. "But even if it is, you're not alone."

CHAPTER 5

Bandages and Burdens

Fiona's home sat at the far end of Waratah Crescent, a sleek, modern creature among Northport's charming old weatherboards and fibro cottages. It looked like the sort of house that had never once known the chaos of misplaced keys or unfolded laundry.

Everything about it was deliberate.

Floor-to-ceiling windows, a minimalist fireplace in the corner, and the kind of backyard that looked professionally trimmed on a weekly schedule. Her couch was firm leather, the rugs from Carpet World, and her two IKEA bookshelves lined neatly with legal texts, thrillers, and one slightly battered copy of Little Women that didn't quite fit but clearly wasn't going anywhere.

And yet tonight, Fiona's meticulously curated living room was once again gloriously invaded by our women, their mismatched mugs, socks, and slippers, and the happy clatter of wine glasses and foil trays. I'd brought leftover apricot tart, still warm, and Naomi was already three spoonfuls into someone else's tiramisu while holding her chipped mug that read World's Best Mum in faded blue paint.

"I swear to God," Naomi was saying, waving her spoon like a weapon, "teenagers are feral. They're like hormonal brush tail possums. I got home last night, and my middle one, Josh, tried to microwave a metal fork. A fork!"

The room groaned in unison, followed by peals of laughter.

"Did it explode?" George asked eagerly, already grinning.

"No," Naomi said, eyes wide. "The microwave did. I'm officially taking him out of my will."

Shanice gasped through her laughter. "I don't know how you do it. Work, kids, all of it. I can barely take care of my dog without losing it."

"Wine. I am so glad we have migrated a bit towards it," Naomi replied, raising her glass in salute. "And the deep, unwavering knowledge that if I drop the ball, no one else is going to pick it up. Single motherhood 101."

We laughed again, but Diana leaned forward, curiosity softening her expression. "But seriously, how do you manage the emotional load? The hours? Doesn't it burn you out?"

Naomi paused. I saw it. That tiny hitch in her smile. The part she tries to keep hidden most of the time.

"I love the work," she said slowly. "Most days. You get to help people. You catch things early. You're useful. You witness people in the rawest moments."

We all grew quiet as her tone changed.

"But sometimes, you miss something."

She stared into her mug as if it might show her the right words.

"There was a patient," she continued. "Olivia. Early forties. Came in one evening, said she had discomfort. Thought it was heartburn. Just wanted to be sure. I told her that a doctor would see her shortly. She said she was in a rush. Didn't want to wait."

Naomi's voice cracked slightly. "She told me she had things to do. Just give me something, she said. I asked a few more questions. Tired, chest discomfort. I figured stress. She had two kids and a mortgage. You know the story."

She swallowed. "Two weeks later, she died. Heart attack. On her son's fifth birthday."

The silence that followed was absolute. Reverent.

"No one blamed me. Not really. But I blamed myself. I still blame myself. Every time someone walks into emergency looking a little off, I think of her."

Vivian's eyes shone with unshed tears. Bethany pressed a hand to her chest.

"I found out where they live. Her husband and the kids," Naomi said, barely above a whisper. "Every month since, I've sent them cash. No note. No return address. Just money. I don't even know if he uses it. I just can't stop. I think if I stop, it'll mean I've moved on. And I'm not ready for that."

Her voice wavered.

"But it's draining me. Financially, emotionally. I'm barely covering the mortgage. My kids think I'm hiding money for a surprise holiday. I lie to them every month."

I reached across the coffee table and rested my hand on her knee. "That's not just guilt, Naomi. That's love. And compassion."

Zoe nodded. "But it's not sustainable. You need someone supporting you, too."

Fiona, quiet until now, leaned back against her couch, arms folded but eyes gentle. "Have you ever thought about telling the husband? Maybe he'd want to know. Maybe he'd be grateful."

Naomi shook her head quickly. "Or maybe he'd hate me."

The silence that followed wasn't uncomfortable. It was contemplative. Each of us privately calculating what we would carry if we were her. What we already were carrying.

"I just wanted to make something right," Naomi said, her voice cracking fully now.

"You did," Bethany whispered. "Even if it doesn't feel like it."

As the night wore on, the mood slowly lifted.

We cried, yes, but we laughed too.

And we all held Naomi a little tighter than usual as we said our goodbyes.

We agreed the next gathering would be at Natalie Cho's place. Vivian would share next time something she had mentioned last week with a tentative look in her eyes.

I watched the women filter out into the cool night air, their arms linked, heads tilted in quiet conversation. Just as I began gathering plates, I saw Fiona press something into Naomi's hand—a plain envelope.

Naomi pulled back. "Fiona, I can't..."

"Don't argue," Fiona said. "Consider it a donation. For your possums."

Naomi laughed, but I saw her wiping her cheek with the back of her hand as she turned away. She wouldn't cry in front of us. But she would once she reached her car.

We all carry something. We all need places to put it down.

Tonight, Naomi found hers. And in some small way, maybe we all did too.

CHAPTER 6

The Call and the Letter

The morning after our gathering, I moved slowly through my quiet little house, the kind of slow that comes from too much red wine and a heart too full. My head was pleasantly fuzzy, but my thoughts were still sharp, flashing with snippets of Naomi's trembling voice, the sound of laughter around Fiona's living room, and all those ridiculous mugs proudly held like totems of identity.

I stood at the kitchen sink rinsing them one by one. Everyone had decided to leave them behind for the next time. Smiling as I recalled George's cartoon koala in downward dog and Naomi's gloriously battered "#MumLife" mug. I could still hear her making us laugh one minute and nearly break the next.

The house creaked beneath my slippers; the timber floors were always honest in the morning light. A soft breeze danced through the lace curtains, bringing with it the scent of jacaranda from the tree just outside. It was the kind of morning that whispered of new beginnings.

Mug in hand, I climbed the stairs slowly, my fingers trailing along the banister. I paused at the end of the hallway and looked towards the door of my study.

A familiar ripple of something.

Eagerness, maybe even excitement, passed through me.

Today, I felt like I could write again.

Since Henry died, writing had become a hollow thing.

I'd tried, of course.

Pages and pages of abandoned scenes, scattered in journals or left to rot in Word documents named "maybe".

It just never came to life the way it used to.

Not without him nearby, turning pages of a newspaper, grunting at headlines, tossing in the occasional dry comment that would have me laughing into my tea.

But last night had stirred something in me.

The confessions.

The honesty.

The ache and beauty of those women, messy and real and trying, just like I was. Real life, I thought, that's the richest soil for a story.

I set down my mug, tucked a stray curl behind my ear, and opened the door to my secret place.

My desk sat in the soft golden light. I cracked my knuckles - some habits never fade - and pulled out a fresh leather-bound notebook.

No more pecking at old outlines.

No more editing the past.

Today, I would begin.

At the top of the page, I scrawled the title that had whispered itself into my mind during the night:

"The Last First Kiss."

The story came to me like a gust of wind.

A vibrant, funny woman in her sixties meets a charming younger man in the most ridiculous way, maybe at a jazz concert, or after spilling coffee on him in the middle of a crowded street. Their chemistry would be instant, inconvenient. Complicated by an estranged daughter, the ghost of a marriage, and some scandal from an old university past.

My pen flew.

The writing that feels like running downhill - fast and free and a little reckless.

I smiled, sipping my coffee. "I'm on fire this morning," I said aloud, amused at my enthusiasm.

I had just written the line "He kissed her like a promise he wasn't sure he could keep..." when the landline rang.

The sudden sound made me jump.

I hadn't realised how still the house had become.

Frowning, I stood, walked across the room, and picked up the receiver.

"Hello?"

Static.

Then silence.

Then — "Mrs Whitman?"

The voice was low.

Male.

Unfamiliar.

My heart thudded. "Speaking."

"You don't know me," he said. "But you knew my father."

I blinked. "I think you've got the wrong number."

"I don't," the voice said gently.

"You were at the University of Sydney. You knew him. You loved him. And he loved you. He never stopped."

My mouth went dry.

"Who was your father?" I asked, my voice cautious.

"You'll find out soon enough," he said. "There's something you need to see. It's about Henry."

Henry.

"My husband?" I whispered.

"Yes. And the life you think you had."

Click.

Just like that, he was gone.

I stood there, the receiver heavy and limp in my hand. The dial tone buzzed like a dull roar in my ears.

Henry.

My Henry.

Gone almost a year now.

My partner, my safe harbour.

The man who left his socks on the floor and made terrible tea, and whom I had loved every day for forty years.

The life you thought you had.

I lowered the phone, missing the cradle on the first try. My fingers were shaking. I pressed a hand to my stomach, which now felt icy and tight.

Back at my desk, my notebook sat open, hopeful and bright and suddenly, achingly naïve.

Of course.

Of course, just as I began to breathe again, the past would come knocking.

I reached for my coffee, took the last sip, wiped my mouth on the sleeve of my cardigan. The familiar gesture steadied me.

There had been whispers over the years.

Little things I'd chosen not to see.

A few odd withdrawals.

A late return from a "conference".

But I'd trusted him.

You knew him.

You loved him.

He loved you.

What was that supposed to mean?

A knock startled me.

Sharp and close.

I blinked, heart racing, and made my way downstairs.

Through the frosted glass, I could just make out a shape. A courier? A visitor? But when I opened the door, no one was there.

Only an envelope.

Small. Square. Heavy.

It sat alone on the doorstep, as if it had fallen from the sky.

I picked it up carefully.

My name was written on the front in a looping, unfamiliar hand.

I turned it over and saw it was sealed with red wax, goodness, an actual wax seal. Who still used those? I muttered under my breath. But then I saw the symbol imprinted in the wax: a tree, with branches tangled around serpents.

It pulsed in my palm.

Inside the house, my novel waited — love, sex, secrets, possibility.

But I already knew nothing I could imagine would compete with what was coming.

I stood there for a long moment, then quietly closed the door.

Back upstairs, the sun had dimmed; the light was cooler now. I placed the envelope on my desk, beside my hopeful little notebook, and reached for the letter opener Henry had given me years ago - a slim, silver blade shaped like a quill.

I sliced it open.

One sheet. Thick, cream-coloured.

Typed.

You loved a man who was not the man you thought he was.

Henry Whitman had secrets.

He left something behind for you, something hidden.

If you want the truth, start at the place where you first said yes.

You'll find the first piece there.

No signature.

No address.

I read it twice, then again.

The place I first said yes.

My mind reeled.

Not our wedding too obvious.

Not the proposal in our kitchen, over burnt toast.

No, before that.

Leura.

A getaway to the Blue Mountains.

Our first weekend away. Just us. A tiny cottage - Willowmere, I think it was called. He asked me to go with him, no promises, just time. And I'd said yes, heart thudding, cheeks flushed.

The cottage.

Could it still be there?

I opened my laptop. Typed in "Leura cottages". I expected little. Businesses closed. Places changed.

But there it was.

Willowmere Cottage.

Established 1927. A rustic retreat for those seeking charm and nostalgia.

And a phone number. I stared at the screen for a long time before I picked up my mobile and dialled. My voice didn't even shake as I made the booking.

Whatever Henry had left for me, whatever truth was hidden in that past, I was going to find it.

Even if it shattered me.

I packed lightly: an overnight bag, a change of clothes, my book, A Night of Love by J. F. Nodar. I grabbed the letter and my notebook, now a strange pairing, and walked downstairs with renewed energy.

In the master bedroom, I glanced at Henry's photo on the mantel, hand hovering.

Not yet. Not until I knew the truth.

Within the hour, I was in the car. Bag beside me. The envelope tucked safely in my purse.

As I passed the butcher's, the bookshop, the café where we'd first gathered, I didn't look back.

Out on the open road, past the last white fences of Northport, I felt something strange.

Not just fear. Not just sorrow.

Something else.

Possibility.

This wasn't just Henry's mystery anymore.

It was mine.

And this time, I wasn't writing a story.

I was living it.

CHAPTER 7

The Place Where She Said Yes

The drive to Leura took longer than I remembered. The highway stretched endlessly ahead, flanked by tall gums swaying under a restless breeze, their shadows flickering like ghosts across the cracked asphalt. I didn't bother with the radio. Normally, I'd have a station on, or maybe a podcast for company, but today I welcomed the silence. The kind that wraps itself around you and forces you to think—maybe even feel.

As the car climbed into the Blue Mountains, a pale mist rolled in, curling low over the trees and folding itself against the road's edge like smoke from a long-forgotten fire. It was mid-afternoon, but the clouds had thickened, dimming the day to a heavy, overcast grey.

I turned off the main road onto a narrow, winding dirt track that snaked through the bush. Gravel crunched beneath the tyres. No signs, no cabins, no other cars. Just me and the trees and whatever waited at the end of this path.

And then I saw it.

Willowmere.

Standing just where it always had, like a memory dredged from a half-dream.

Only now smaller. Sadder.

The years had not been kind. Weather and time had bleached the timber silver. The front verandah sagged dangerously in places. Spiderweb cracks spread across several windowpanes. Ivy climbed unapologetically up one side, vanishing into the roofline as if it had taken permanent residence.

Still, it was unmistakable.

The battered wooden sign still hung from its rusted chain, WILLOWMERE, creaking faintly in the wind.

And of course, I could hear Henry's voice as clear as day.

"C'mon, Ellie. It's not in disrepair. It's character."

I swallowed the lump rising in my throat. I grabbed my bag and stepped out into the cool, damp air. The mist kissed my face like a secret.

The key was exactly where the woman from the booking service had said it would be—under the old terracotta frog pot by the door. I fumbled with the swollen lock until the door groaned open, reluctantly yielding to my push.

The scent inside hit me like a memory: damp timber, old dust, and something faintly metallic—like the echo of forgotten stories.

The cottage was as I half remembered it: a narrow living room with a worn stone fireplace, two threadbare armchairs, and a battered coffee table. Beyond that, a tight little kitchen and a bedroom that looked just big enough to turn around in.

Time had touched everything, worn it down—but not without dignity. There was something gentle about the decay, as if the place had grown old waiting for someone to remember it.

I placed my bag just inside the door and stood still for a moment.

Now what?

There were no instructions. No map. Just the cryptic words from a stranger and a letter full of riddles.

But I've spent my life buried in books—tangled in metaphor, decoding secrets hidden in footnotes and silence. I know how to read between the lines.

"Start at the place where you first said yes."

It wasn't just the cottage. It was here. That night by the fire, the smell of cheap Shiraz and Henry's rough hands wrapping around mine. That moment when I let go of the life I thought I was supposed to want and chose the one I could only just imagine.

I turned towards the fireplace.

It was squat, built from mottled stone. The mantel bore old scars from heat and smoke. Above it hung a painting I vaguely remembered—a misty riverbank, its colours now muted into near oblivion.

And then I saw it.

A tiny gap in the stonework. Just wide enough to slip a fingertip into.

My heart thumped.

I crouched down, pressed my fingers against the edge. The stone didn't budge at first. I pushed harder. A low grinding sound groaned through the silence, and the stone shifted—just enough to reveal a narrow cavity.

With trembling hands, I reached in.

My fingers brushed something hard, cold, and wrapped in old cloth. Carefully, I pulled it free.

A rusted tin box. The kind my grandfather used to keep screws in. It was wrapped in a stained scrap of kitchen towel that smelled faintly of earth, time, and perhaps something else—something buried.

I knelt on the hearth, laid the box in front of me, and peeled back the cloth. The lid creaked as I pried it open.

Inside were three items:

A small black notebook, cracked and weathered.

A delicate gold locket, tarnished but still gleaming beneath the dust.

And a folded photograph, curled at the edges with age.

I reached for the photo first.

It was black and white. A little blurry.

Henry.

Much younger.

Laughing.

With his arm around another man, I didn't recognise.

They stood in front of a battered old pickup truck—and behind them, unmistakably, were the shattered windows of a Commonwealth Bank branch.

Police officers in the background.

Sirens frozen in time.

My chest tightened.

A robbery?

No. No.

He couldn't have?

I set the photo down with shaking hands and picked up the locket.

It clicked open under my thumb.

Inside were two faces I didn't know: a woman, smiling softly, and a baby.

I could feel my reality shifting beneath me.

I opened the notebook last. Henry's handwriting. Rushed. Unfiltered. Filled with scrawled entries, some barely legible.

"I told her half the truth. The rest she wouldn't forgive. If it ever comes to light, she deserves to know it was never about love. She was my salvation. The bank job... not what it seemed. They lied. We all did. For Eleanor: When the time comes, follow the trail. Find the truth. Forgive me if you can."

I pressed my hand to my mouth. The tears burned but didn't fall. Not yet.

A robbery.

A child.

A woman I'd never known.

And Henry, confessing with ink and silence what he never could with words.

I sat there, surrounded by the puzzle he'd left me. The tin, the locket, the photo, the notebook—all spread across the hearth like clues from a novel I didn't remember agreeing to star in.

Outside, the mist thickened, and the last light vanished.

When the mantel clock struck six, I stood slowly. My knees ached. My heart more.

I wrapped everything back in the towel, tucked it into my bag, and stood staring into the dark.

Someone knew about Henry's past.

Someone had wanted me to find this.

And whether it shattered the life we'd built together or not, I had to see it through.

I will go home tomorrow.

And then I would start digging.

CHAPTER 8

Shadows and Lights

The next afternoon, I left Willowmere behind. The mist had lifted slightly, revealing pale patches of sky between the trees, but everything still felt subdued. As I wound back through the mountain roads, the quiet countryside rolled past like a fading dream. The drive home felt longer than the drive there, heavier. The kind of heavy that settled in your chest and didn't lift, no matter how many times you opened a window or changed posture.

Every few minutes, I glanced at the passenger seat.

The bag sat there silently. But I could hear the faint rattle of the tin box inside every time the car hit a bump. It sounded like a secret trying to escape.

By the time I hit the familiar edges of Sydney, a knot had wound itself so tightly in my chest I could barely take a full breath. My thoughts spiralled. The photograph. The locket. Henry's handwriting.

I needed air.

I needed a distraction. Something normal. Something grounding.

And then I remembered—the Northport Coffee Group was meeting tonight. But where?

I couldn't, for the life of me, remember the location. I pulled over near a petrol station and scrolled through my phone, searching for Natalie Cho's number. Sweet, thoughtful Natalie. Quiet, precise, and more organised than all of us combined. If anyone knew where we were meant to be tonight, it was her.

She picked up after two rings, her voice calm but just slightly breathless—like she'd been chasing after something, or someone.

"Hi Natalie, it's Eleanor," I said, trying to sound a bit more composed than I felt. "Sorry to bother you, but could you remind me where we're meeting tonight?"

"Oh, of course!" she said brightly. "It's actually at my place this time. Six o'clock. I'll text you the address now."

"Perfect, thank you. I might be a little late—I'm not quite back in Northport yet. Just have to stop at home first."

"Not to worry, Eleanor," she said. "We'll have wine waiting."

I laughed softly and thanked her, then merged back onto the motorway heading towards Jacaranda Street, tapping the steering wheel to keep myself grounded. "Long day," I murmured aloud.

A few minutes later, my phone buzzed with her address, and I couldn't help but smile. These women, this mismatched tribe of hearts and chaos—they were becoming something real to me. Something solid. And tonight, I needed that.

I arrived home just after five. I freshened up, changed clothes, and, on impulse, grabbed a bottle of Shiraz before heading back out. As I pulled up in front of Natalie's cottage, the sun was hanging low behind the trees like a slow, golden coin being tucked away for the night.

Her house was a charming weatherboard with a wide verandah wrapped in climbing jasmine. Light spilled from the windows, and I could hear laughter before I even reached the steps.

I took a breath, smoothed my hair, and made my way to the door.

Inside, the scene was delightfully chaotic—our kind of chaos. Women sprawled across armchairs, couches, beanbags. Mugs in every hand, pastries disappearing from a plate that had clearly already been raided. The air smelled of vanilla and spice and comfort.

Naomi waved me over as I slipped in, gesturing to a spot between George and Fiona. I settled in just as Vivian Mendez spoke.

"Photography has always helped me make sense of things," she said, standing near the fireplace, a stack of photos fanned out behind her. "When you grow up moving between homes, between people, you realise pictures are the only proof you existed somewhere."

The room hushed. Not out of awkwardness—out of reverence. Even Bea, usually quick with a snarky quip, stayed silent.

Vivian held up a photo—a black-and-white shot of an empty swing, mid-sway, in an abandoned playground. Stark. Lonely. Haunting.

"I enjoy capturing what people don't notice," she continued. "The in-between moments."

She picked up another photo—a self-portrait reflected in a rainy window, her face fractured and blurred by droplets.

"I've spent a lot of time alone," she said softly. "Sometimes by choice. Sometimes not."

I felt something shift in my chest. That ache again. That deep, quiet grief you recognise only when you see someone else holding it.

Vivian looked down at her feet, then took a deep breath. "I came to Northport looking for something. Maybe... someone."

A ripple of energy moved through the room. Every woman sat a little straighter. My hands curled in my lap.

Vivian's voice cracked, but she kept going. "Joining this group wasn't random. I needed a place to land. I didn't come here to lie, but... I didn't exactly come in clean, either. I think I found more than I was expecting."

Her gaze skimmed the room—and then paused. On me.

Just a moment.

Barely a second longer than polite.

But it felt like the world had tilted.

She dropped her eyes quickly and added, "I hope you'll let me stay, even if I started with secrets."

The room went still again. We were always good at holding space for the hard things.

Then Naomi leaned forward, grinning wide. "Well, hell, Viv. If we kicked out everyone here who started off with a secret, we'd be sitting around sipping coffee by ourselves."

Laughter bubbled up, a little cautious at first, but genuine.

George reached over and patted Vivian's knee. "Too late. You're one of us now, whether or not you like it."

Vivian smiled—shaky, but real. Fiona muttered something about needing emergency wine, and Natalie and Zoe headed for the kitchen to grab another bottle.

I sat quietly in the corner, trying to steady my breathing. My heart had started thudding in a way that was no longer about nerves. It was something older. Deeper.

Vivian hadn't said it outright. But my instincts—the same ones that had served me through a lifetime of literature and buried truths—were screaming.

Could it be?

Could she be my daughter?

The child I gave up a lifetime ago?

The thought made me dizzy. But I didn't move. I didn't let it show.

Vivian still had more to say.

"I guess what I'm trying to say," she added, "is sometimes family isn't about blood. It's about who shows up. Who listens, who chooses you, even after they've seen the mess."

A soft murmur of agreement passed through the room.

My throat tightened.

Then—she looked at me.

Really looked.

And for one fragile second, something passed between us.

Recognition? Hope? A question neither of us had the words for yet?

I smiled—just the tiniest twitch of my lips. She smiled back.

The rest of the night was filled with exactly the chatter I needed: bad date stories, tragic baking attempts, teenage dramas, and someone misplacing their keys for the third time this week. It was messy, and honest, and ordinary.

Shanice and Beatrice both rushed to volunteer their stories for the next time. I offered to host again. More coffee. More wine. More space for secrets to rise and settle.

As I sat among these brilliant, beautiful, complicated women, one thought circled endlessly through my mind:

First, Henry's secret. Now Vivian's.

The past never stays buried. Not really.

Especially when it shows up on your doorstep... holding a camera... and a thousand unspoken questions.

CHAPTER 9

Cracks in the Armour

The plates of pastries had been reduced to nothing but a few flaky crumbs. Most of the mugs were forgotten now, replaced by wineglasses that glinted softly in the candlelight. "When did we start with more wine?" I thought.

Around me, the warm hum of conversation drifted like a breeze through Natalie's jasmine-scented home.

I sat quietly, hands wrapped around a cooling cup of coffee I had no intention of drinking, my thoughts split between the here and now and the rusted tin box still tucked away back home. Every so often, I'd catch a phrase or a laugh and smile, but truthfully, my heart hadn't quite caught up to the room.

And then Vivian.

She shifted across the circle, just slightly, and then made her way over, settling on the floor beside my chair. She said nothing at first. Just folded her legs beneath her, set her glass of wine carefully on the floor, and offered me a small, tentative smile.

I smiled back, and my pulse did something stupid and traitorous in my chest.

It was such a small thing. Hardly noticeable to anyone else. But to me, it was everything. Her nearness was a soft, silent presence, a question, a whisper, a crack in the wall I'd built over decades.

Before either of us could speak, Bea clapped her hands once—loud and sudden—and the room turned toward her like sunflowers chasing light.

"All right, ladies," she announced with a wicked grin, curls bouncing. "Since our dear Viv here kicked off the truth parade, Shanice and I are up next."

A round of teasing applause rippled through the group.

Shanice, glamorous and cool even in ripped jeans and a vintage Bowie tee, groaned theatrically. "Oh God, Bea. Don't make it sound like we're being sacrificed."

"Please," Bea said, flicking a grape into her mouth with alarming precision. "Confession is just yoga for the soul. Hurts like hell, but afterward? Nirvana."

Laughter bubbled up, easing the lingering weight in the room.

Shanice rolled her eyes and pulled her dark curls into a messy knot. "Fine. But you go first, Yogi Bear."

Bea gave a mock bow, then perched on the edge of the nearest chair. Her eyes, usually full of mischief, had taken on a different sheen. Something quieter. Braver.

"Well," she began, "most of you know me as the woman who cracks jokes at entirely the wrong time and stretches in supermarket aisles."

There were soft chuckles and nods.

"But what you don't know," she said, voice softening, "is that I'm in love with someone I have absolutely no business loving."

A hush fell over us.

I saw Fiona stiffen ever so slightly. Natalie's hand froze, a pastry half-lifted to her mouth.

Bea smirked faintly. "And no, don't worry, it's not any of your husbands."

Nervous laughter trickled through the room.

"It's my best friend's husband," she continued. "Has been for years."

A sharp inhale, a flicker of movement from Vivian beside me.

"I didn't mean for it to happen," Bea said. "But he listens. He laughs at my bad jokes. He buys my dog birthday gifts. And one day, I just realised I was in love."

She twisted the hem of her linen pants between her fingers.

"And the worst part? I think he feels it too."

No one spoke. We didn't have to. The weight of her words had settled over us like a heavy blanket.

Bea sat up straighter. "But I'd never act on it. Never. Because she's, my friend. And he's not mine to love."

Naomi leaned in, her voice low but sure. "That's brave as hell, Bea."

Bea laughed, teary-eyed, brushing her cheek. "Or just really, really stupid."

"No," Natalie whispered. "It's called being loyal."

Bea smiled then. A real one. Crooked and beautiful. Shanice reached over and took her hand, and something unspoken passed between them that only women like us understand.

I felt Vivian shift beside me. Not away. Closer.

As if the gravity between us had grown stronger in the silence.

Then Shanice groaned. "Well, after that, my story's going to sound like a bad soap opera."

George raised her glass. "Honey, we live for soap operas."

Shanice laughed nervously. "Okay. So, most of you know I've been dating two guys."

There were immediate catcalls and exaggerated gasps.

"What you don't know," she said, her cheeks turning a deep red, "is that I'm pregnant. And I don't know which one is the father."

Even the candle on the coffee table seemed to pause.

"I wasn't planning this," she rushed on. "I've been so focused on building my brand, launching the line. Kids weren't even in the plan yet."

Her hands twisted in her lap, tugging at the denim fabric as if it could anchor her.

"And now I don't even know how to tell them. Either of them. I'm scared. Of everything. What if they both leave? What if the wrong one stays?"

I watched her, this bold, luminous woman, suddenly so raw and uncertain.

Bea touched her shoulder. "Whatever happens, we're here. You've got us."

Shanice blinked hard. "Thanks. I just needed to say it. Out loud."

Naomi snorted softly. "Half of us wouldn't exist if life went according to plan."

Laughter rose again.

Gentler this time.

Real.

Vivian leaned her head softly against my armchair. A subtle, tender weight. So natural, it nearly undid me.

I wanted to reach out. Touch her hair. Say something. Anything.

But I stayed still.

Instead, I let the quiet hope bloom inside me, warm and dangerous and unbearably fragile.

The night spun on in gentle circles—more stories, more wine, minor victories, and quiet truths.

And as I looked around at the women laughing, crying, teasing each other over burnt lasagna and failed Tinder dates, I realised something that struck me in my chest:

This is family.

Not the posed, tidy, Christmas card kind.

This was better.

It was complicated, unfinished, generous. It held space for secrets, for second chances.

And for the first time in a long while, I felt like I might belong to something again.

Vivian glanced up, her eyes searching.

They met mine.

A spark passed between us.

Not yet.

But soon.

As the evening drew to a close and everyone began gathering their things, someone mentioned returning to Natalie's for the next meeting, and everyone eagerly agreed. Chairs scraped. Mugs clinked. The air was thick with vanilla and laughter and something sacred.

I was slipping on my cardigan when I felt a hand brush lightly against mine.

Vivian.

"Thanks for tonight," she said, her voice quiet. Just for me.

"It meant more than you know."

I squeezed her hand gently. "You're not alone anymore, Viv. None of us are."

She gave me a smile—crooked, brilliant, and just a little broken—and then slipped into the night with the others.

I stayed behind a moment longer, letting the sounds of dishes and departing footsteps fade, letting myself breathe.

The scent of candle wax and coffee lingered, grounding me.

Maybe, I thought, maybe forgiveness wasn't just a story I told other people. Maybe I could write a new chapter, even for myself.

But tomorrow I'd begin again. I needed to return to the past. I needed to uncover what Henry had left behind at Willowmere.

Tonight was about healing.

Tomorrow would be for truth.

CHAPTER 10

Ghosts of Mason Creek

I opened my eyes before the sun had bothered to rise. For a while, I just lay there in bed, listening to the quiet stirrings of a Northport morning—the bark of the neighbour's overly enthusiastic terrier, the scrape of metal as someone dragged their bin to the curb. When I finally glanced at the clock, it blinked back at me: 5:17 AM.

"God, I hate being old," I muttered to the ceiling.

With a sigh, I swung my legs out of bed and slipped into my cardigan, the one that smelled faintly of jasmine and coffee and had become my unofficial uniform. The floor was cold beneath my feet as I padded into the kitchen. Even the air still held traces of yesterday—the earthy scent of leftover coffee grounds and the faint sweetness from the garden blooming just beyond the back door.

I made my coffee the way I always had: a scoop of Moccona French Roast, four spoons of sugar (yes, four), and a wait for the kettle's familiar hiss. When it boiled, I poured the water with care, stirring slowly until the cup steamed like an offering.

With the mug nestled in my hands, I climbed the stairs and opened the study door.

The biscuit tin was still there, sitting on the desk as if it hadn't moved in years. Its painted roses were so faded they were almost ghosts now. I set the coffee down beside it and sat heavily, letting the silence wrap around me.

I ran a thumb along the edge of the tin. Then I opened it.

Inside—just as I had left them—were the relics of a life I no longer fully understood.

The notebook came first. Henry's notebook. Its spine cracked, edges frayed, the ink fading in places. I flipped through it again, eyes scanning the pages filled with scattered thoughts, strange initials, half-maps, cryptic notes. I stopped on one page:

"Willowmere."
"Spring Fair '94."
"M.C."

The locket came next. Still warm from sitting inside the tin, still tarnished, but no less beautiful. I opened it again and stared at the two tiny photos tucked inside—me and Henry, decades ago. I hadn't even known this picture existed. Had he carried it with him? Or hidden it away for me to find?

And finally—the photograph. The one that cracked everything open.

Younger Henry. A woman I didn't recognise. Laughing eyes. Dark hair tumbled over her shoulders. A baby in her arms.

There was nothing written on the back. No names. No date.

But my gut already knew—this wasn't a photo taken in passing. It meant something.

I stared at it for a long moment, then whispered to the empty room, "What are you trying to tell me, Henry?"

Leaving my coffee to cool, I opened my laptop. Northport's internet groaned awake begrudgingly, and I began what I'd always been good at—research. I took out my notebook and made a timeline, cross-referencing everything I'd uncovered:

1973: Spring Fair – Henry worked a booth.
1994: Willowmere – a cryptic reference.
M.C. – a mystery still unsolved.

I dug into online archives, old newspaper scans, anything from 1973. I found a blurry image in a local article—Henry, young and grinning, standing beside a booth for the Mason Creek Charity Raffle.

Mason Creek.
M.C.

It was only 27 kilometres from Northport.
A spark flared inside me. I scribbled furiously.
Then, just as I started searching Mason Creek's charity and adoption records, the landline rang.
I jumped. No one ever called this early.
"Who the hell..." I muttered, grabbing the receiver.
"Hello?"

A pause.

Breathing.

Then a voice—low, male, deliberate.

"You're closer than you think, Eleanor."

I went cold. "Who is this?"

"A friend. Look at the photograph. The one in the tin. Look at the background."

I turned, heart hammering.

"What do you want from me?"

"To finish what Henry started. Find her before they do."

Click, and the line went dead.

I stood there, hand still clutched around the receiver, with a strange buzzing in my ears.

Then I walked back to the study, legs trembling slightly.

I picked up the photo. The woman. The baby. Henry.

I fumbled for my magnifying glass—an old habit from my years of poring over archival manuscripts—and held it up to the image.

There. In the background.

A banner. Faded but still legible.

Mason Creek Spring Festival 1973.

And beneath it, in smaller print:

Sponsored by Willowmere Home for Unwed Mothers.

Willowmere.

Henry hadn't just known the place. He'd been involved.

My heart beat harder now, not just with fear—but with purpose.

I scribbled more notes, then looked at the clock: 6:39 AM.

I would go to Mason Creek today.

By 8:27 AM, I was on the road. My thermos sat beside me, cooling in the passenger seat as I gripped the steering wheel and drove.

When I passed the welcome sign—Mason Creek: Est. 1864 – A Proud Community—a familiar unease settled in my stomach.

The town looked untouched by time. Quiet, aging storefronts. A barbershop pole still spins in the breeze.

And then I saw it.

Willowmere.

The old home stood like a ghost at the edge of town. Ivy climbing its sides, windows boarded or broken, the sign at the gate swinging lazily.

I pulled over and sat there for a long breath.

Then I got out.

The gate groaned as I opened it. No cars. No sound. Even the birds seemed to avoid the place.

I knocked on the front door, hoping against reason that someone might answer.

And then—

"You are looking for someone?"

The voice startled me.

CHAPTER 11

New Beginning

I was fifteen kilometres from Northport when I changed the playlist for the third time, hoping something—classical, jazz, even guilty-pleasure pop—might help quiet my thoughts. But the fog in my mind was stubborn, and the further I drove from Mason Creek, the heavier it pressed on my chest. The sign for Northport loomed like a familiar gatekeeper. Home. Comforting, yes—but also a reminder of the mess I had to untangle.

My phone buzzed, flashing a name across the car's screen.

Vivien – Starling Press.

I groaned and then forced my voice into something resembling cheerful. "Vivien, how lovely to hear your voice. I was just thinking about you."

"Uh-huh," came the unimpressed reply. "I've been thinking about you, too. Specifically, about the manuscript you promised me last month. So where exactly are we with Barefoot in the Vineyard?"

I blinked and then gave my head a slow shake. I couldn't even fake it.

"Nowhere. The vineyard is barren. The barefoot woman has grown boots and taken off. I can't write it, Vivien."

A long, silence-padded pause.

"Are you seriously telling me you've got writer's block again?"

"No," I sighed. "I'm telling you I have writer's exhaustion."

She made a dramatic sound only Vivien could pull off. "So, what are you proposing now? A six-month delay?"

"I have an idea," I said carefully, almost cautiously.

"Oh, Lord," she muttered.

"No, really. Just listen. I've been sitting in on these weekly coffee group gatherings—Northport women, the ones I mentioned. They're funny, complicated, and their stories are astonishing. I want to write about that."

"You want to do what?" she asked, already suspicious.

"A collection of interwoven short stories. Fictionalised, of course. Inspired by these women—their confessions, regrets, jokes, triumphs. Think Olive Kitteridge meets The Best Exotic Marigold Hotel. No vineyard seductions. Just genuine stories."

Another pause.

"So, you want to ditch a surefire bestseller to write a book about chatty women and their emotional breakthroughs over lattes?"

I smiled. "They're not lonely, Vivien. We have each other."

She exhaled, but there was something softer behind the sound now. "You're a talented writer, Eleanor. But this is a risk."

"I know. But I need it. And I think the readers might too."

She hesitated. Then said, "Fine. No promises. But if—and I do mean if—you finish it and I don't hate it, I'll bring it to marketing. Deal?"

"Deal."

"And Eleanor? No more vineyard women with selective amnesia, okay? That trope's dead."

I laughed and ended the call just as I turned onto my street. I dropped my suitcase inside the front door, changed clothes quickly, and drove to the Northport Coffee House.

My usual table by the window was mercifully free. I ordered a flat white, opened my laptop, and typed a tentative working title: Latte Ladies.

The ideas were already trickling in—Beatrice and her story about chasing an emu with a wheelbarrow, Natalie, and her cryptic remarks about her missing husband, Fiona's gambling exploits that always ended in drama and laughter. But even as the fiction bloomed, a real thread still tugged at me.

Margaret Clarke.

Henry's past was no longer a closed book—it was a half-burned manuscript with missing pages. And Margaret... she might be the key to everything.

I opened a new tab and started with the obvious: White Pages. Typed "Margaret Clarke," narrowed by age range and region—Henry had mentioned Victoria once, maybe Bendigo.

Pages of results.

I panned through them like a miner searching for gold in a river of identical stones. Nothing helpful.

I moved on to LinkedIn. True Local. Dead ends.

Facebook gave me a strange collection: one Margaret Clarke with a cat in a tiara, another posting about mushrooms with the caption "Nature's treasures!" Lovely, but not useful.

My coffee had gone lukewarm by then.

"I need something more professional," I muttered, rubbing my temples.

I tried the births, deaths, marriages databases. Found several Margaret Clarkes born in the right decade. One death notice from 2001 in Ballarat. Could it be her? I didn't know.

I jotted it all down in my notebook, then leant back.

If Margaret had changed her name, married, or simply vanished—as people sometimes do—I'd need help. A private investigator, maybe. But I wasn't ready to part with money just yet.

"Let's try the old-fashioned route first," I said aloud.

The next morning, I walked to the Northport Advertiser. The clerk, all eyebrows, and elbows, looked like he'd been surprised in 1986 and had never quite recovered.

"I'd like to place a classified ad," I said.

He blinked. "We don't get many of those anymore. Mostly just lost cats and used Corollas."

"This one's different." I handed over my printed copy.

CHAPTER 12

Zoe's Discovery

I was just reaching for a copy of The Last Migration by Charlotte McConaghy at the local bookshop when I nearly collided with Zoe.

Literally.

One more step and I'd have sloshed my water bottle all over both of us.

"Oh, sorry!" I blurted, juggling the stack of books in my arms.

She blinked. "Eleanor?"

"Zoe? Wow. I didn't expect to see you here."

She gave me a smile that looked more like a hairline fracture. "Yeah, you know. Life. Busy as ever."

I tilted my head. "That's a very rehearsed answer."

She hesitated, then glanced over her shoulder toward the children's section. "Do you have a minute? Maybe we could get a coffee?"

"I was heading to the Northport Café anyway," I said. "Too much caffeine, too little inspiration."

We ended up in a quiet corner of the café, the scent of fresh pastry and brewing beans wrapping around us like a familiar coat.

I stirred my flat white absently while Zoe stared into her chai like she was trying to cast a spell.

Then, softly, she said it.

"I followed Paul to Melbourne."

I looked up, and she held my gaze. Steady. Unflinching.

"I found out he has a second family."

The spoon in my hand stilled.

I didn't speak.

I didn't have the words yet.

"I wasn't sure at first," she said, her voice even. "But now I am. There's a woman. A child. I saw them. I saw him."

I set the spoon down gently. "Zoe..."

"Please don't give me the pity face," she said. "I'm not looking for sympathy. I just needed someone who can listen without trying to fix it."

"Got it," I said quietly. "Still, I'm sorry. That's an awful thing to carry."

"I won't carry it for long," she said, her spine straightening.

"I've decided. I'm going to stay for now. Smile. Pretend. Play the long game. If Paul's going to destroy our marriage, I want to be the one who writes the ending. Not him."

That made me pause.

"You're not going to confront him?"

"Not yet," she said. "I've spent too many years building this life. I won't let it collapse while I'm still inside it."

I nodded slowly. "That sounds calculated."

"It has to be."

I looked at her then-not at the woman who made perfect canapés for our Thursday meetups or who always wore just the right earrings—but at someone who was made of steel beneath the silk. "You're braver than I would be."

She gave me a crooked smile.

"You've got your own mystery, don't you? I saw your ad in the Advertiser, the one about Margaret Clarke."

I blinked. "You saw that?"

"Small town. Everyone sees everything."

I hesitated.

"I'm trying to find her. She might be connected to something I'm writing and something else. I don't quite know what yet. It's either a plot or a puzzle, but I can't leave it alone."

Zoe nodded. "Funny how we end up chasing ghosts, one way or another."

I let out a laugh that surprised even me. "Vivien, my publisher, wants another steamy vineyard novel. But I've got nothing left to say about passion and wine cellars. Lately, real life feels far more tangled than any fiction I've written."

"Maybe you should write about that," she said.

"Maybe I will," I murmured.

We sat in silence, sipping our drinks, letting the quiet settle between us like dust in golden light. Outside, the town moved on.

Dogs tugging leashes, schoolkids pedalling hard, a bus hissing as it came to a stop across the road.

"You know," Zoe said at last, "I have told no one this. Not really. Not even when I suspected. But it feels different with you."

"I'm glad you told me," I said. "And when I figure out what Margaret Clarke means to me, maybe I'll tell you more, too."

She smiled. This time it reached her eyes. "Deal."

We parted at the corner.

Zoe headed toward the butcher, me toward the library.

From a distance, we looked like any two women crossing paths in a small town. But I knew better.

Zoe was building something.

Not with Paul but beyond him. A quiet reinvention.

And I, for all my wandering thoughts and dead husbands and unfinished novels, found myself thinking less about Margaret Clarke and more about Zoe's steady resolve.

What kind of strength did it take to stare betrayal in the face and not flinch?

We both walked into our separate lives carrying the invisible.

Secrets.

Wounds.

Blueprints for survival.

In Northport, nothing stayed buried forever.

Not the truth.

Not betrayal.

Not even the kind of pain that makes you want to disappear.

And if I've learned anything from the women I've come to know, it's that sometimes, it's in the unspoken moments-over coffee, wine, books, or silence, where our genuine stories begin.

CHAPTER 13

Naomi's Burden

Naomi told me everything over lukewarm tea at my kitchen table. Hands trembling slightly, voice steady in that way grief sometimes is when it's had too much time to settle. She had stood at the cemetery gates that morning, she said, letting the wind pull at her like it had a right to. She hadn't fought it. She hadn't felt she deserved comfort.

It had been exactly one year since Olivia Harper had died in the ICU.

One year since Naomi signed the charts, missed a change in vitals.

Subtle, but maybe significant.

The review board called it a cascade of complications, a tragedy no one could have stopped.

But Naomi believed otherwise.

"I should've caught it," she whispered. "I had control. And I lost it."

She said she'd been sending money ever since. Half her pay, quietly, through anonymous accounts. School supplies. Medical debts. Groceries. She'd never signed her name. Never wanted them to know. Her penance was privacy.

That morning had been her ritual: lilies in hand, a stop at Olivia's grave.

But when she arrived, they were already there.

Michael Harper, older than Naomi remembered, stood with his son, Eli. The boy had placed a Lego figure at the base of the headstone. Naomi said she nearly collapsed when she heard him call Michael "Dad."

She didn't speak to them.

She didn't reveal herself.

Just watched from behind a hedge of camellias.

"They're okay," she told me, eyes shining but unshed. "He smiled at the boy. And the boy was talking to Olivia as if she were still part of their day. Like she hadn't been stolen from them."

She could have stepped forward, she said.

Could've dropped to her knees and confessed.

But she didn't.

And I understood that, in the way you understand things that live in your bones. She wasn't trying to unburden herself. She was trying not to ruin what healing they'd found.

When Michael and Eli left, Naomi went to the gravesite and placed the lilies. Whispered a hello. And left.

I sat quietly as she spoke, not touching my tea, not interrupting. There are moments when silence is more generous than speech.

And this was one of them.

Later, she told me she had thought about bringing it up again at the Coffee Group meeting.

The whole truth.

Not names or dates.

Just the question: how do you tell the truth when it might undo the healing you've helped create from the shadows?

That question lingered between us long after she left.

I imagined her driving home. I pictured her townhouse in twilight, her laptop blinking open to a spreadsheet of anonymous generosity. A tally of guilt disguised as good. She had even taken a second job just to keep it going.

It wasn't self-sacrifice.

It was survival.

Her own way of making something grow from soil salted with sorrow.

And I wondered: was anonymous good really good enough?

When I walked her to the door, she said maybe she'd share it again at the next get-together. Maybe she wouldn't.

I didn't press her.

Some stories need to be carried for a while before they're spoken aloud.

Others slip out when no one expects them to. And some, like Naomi's, sit curled in the quiet, waiting for the right breath of courage to unfurl.

That night, I stood at my study window, watching the wind stir the gum trees beyond the porch. I thought of Naomi, her eyes shadowed with responsibility. I thought of Olivia Harper, whose surname I hadn't known until today, and of a child who brought Lego pieces to a grave because he believed they kept his mother close.

In a town like Northport, secrets don't stay buried forever.

They shift.

They breathe.

Sometimes they bloom into truth, painful and necessary.

And sometimes they bring us back to ourselves.

CHAPTER 14

Vivian's Investigation

I didn't mean for it to become an obsession. At first, it was nothing more than an instinct, a flicker of something I'd long buried sparking to life. An old reflex from my years in academia, where I'd chase an unanswered question down every rabbit hole until it gave itself up. But this wasn't a research project. This wasn't a chapter in a dusty manuscript. This was something else.

This was mine.

Vivian Mendez.

The name meant nothing to me at first.

A local photographer, bright, curious, a little guarded behind the eyes.

She joined the Northport Coffee Group not long after I started it. Said she needed inspiration for her next project. But there was a deliberateness to her, a way she'd study the room between sips of chai, linger her gaze on certain photos or objects in my home a moment too long.

At first, I told myself I was imagining it.

Writers have a tendency to fill in blanks with drama.

I saw things that weren't there. But then there were the little coincidences. Her features — dark hair, straight nose, a delicate jawline that mirrored mine too closely to dismiss.

And her eyes.

Deep, brown, searching.

Not unlike my own.

Not unlike the eyes I saw in the mirror when I was young.

Then came the elephant.

A small ceramic elephant I keep on the mantel. Pale blue, chipped ear. I've had it for years. I'm not even sure where I got it anymore — only that I've never been able to part with it. When Vivian's eyes landed on it that day, I saw something change in her. A momentary freeze, then a flicker of recognition. She tried to cover it, but I noticed.

Of course I did.

Writers always notice the flickers.

And then she lingered after the others left.

She insisted on helping with the dishes, even when I waved her off. We moved around each other in a rhythm that unsettled me.

Too fluid, too easy, too familiar.

Like muscle memory from a life, I'd forgotten.

Afterwards, I stepped away to take a phone call, something mundane, a reminder from the chemist, I think, and when I returned, she was standing near the bookshelf, smiling, a little too still. I thought little of it at the time. But later, when I sat down to write, something in me itched. A sense of absence, of being studied. Of the space in my home, not quite as I'd left it.

That night, I barely slept. I lay in bed thinking of the photograph tucked behind the books.

An old one, nearly forgotten, of a newborn wrapped in pink, barely a day old. I hadn't seen it in years, yet I remembered it with vivid clarity. I remembered her.

And the choice I made.

The silence I'd lived with ever since.

I tried to write, but nothing came. Not about vineyards or barefoot women or quiet small towns. All I could think about was Vivian. Her eyes, her laugh, the way she tensed slightly every time someone mentioned family.

She suspects.

Or maybe she knows.

And the truth is, I'm not sure what I want.

To be found?

To be forgiven?

To remain in hiding just a little longer?

The next day, I spotted her again in the CBD, just outside the bookshop. She waved, casual as anything, and I smiled in return. But my chest ached.

She looked so much like someone I'd once imagined my daughter might grow up to be.

Did she know I was watching her walk away? Did she feel the tremor in me when we hugged goodbye?

Later that night, I imagined her at home, sorting through photographs on her laptop, piecing things together. I saw her comparing the baby picture with the one she kept tucked away.

I imagined her calling her adoptive mother — Maria Mendez, yes; I remembered now. A kind woman, always soft-spoken in the adoption records. The sort of woman I once prayed could love my child the way I never could at the time.

If she knew the truth now, what would she do with it?

What would I do?

I walked through my house in the quiet, pausing at the elephant. I picked it up. Ran my thumb over the chipped ear. The weight of it in my hand made my knees weak. What are the odds? What is the line between coincidence and destiny?

I found my notebook and tried to write a letter.

I didn't know what to say.

Dear Vivian,

There is something I need to tell you. Something I should have said the moment I met you...

No.

I think I may be your mother.

Too much.

Too raw.

Too late.

I tore it up and poured myself a glass of wine.

Maybe I would say nothing.

Maybe I'd wait.

Let her come to me.

Maybe she already was.

At the next Coffee Group, I'll watch her again. Not out of fear this time, but hope. Hope that I might one day find the courage to say the words she deserves to hear. Not because I owe her answers, but because I've carried the silence long enough.

This isn't just her story to discover.

It's mine to claim.

CHAPTER 15

The Call and the Confession

I typed the email faster than I usually allow myself to. No edits. No rereads. Highly uncharacteristic. But I was too jittery to worry about second drafts.

Subject: RE: Margaret Clarke
Dear Mr or Ms Tremayne,
Thank you so much for your message. I would be grateful to speak with you directly. Please call my mobile: 0402 984 086. I'm available for most of the day tomorrow.
Kind regards,
Eleanor Whitman

I hit send, my heart fluttering like a moth at a porch light.

It was Wednesday afternoon, and tomorrow the Coffee Group was meeting at my place. I'd already spent most of the morning in a flurry of illogical panic—polishing cutlery no one would notice, vacuuming rugs with monastic fury, and baking three cakes (because clearly one would've been a personal failure). But the email I'd just sent buzzed louder in my brain than the hoover I'd wrangled across the hallway.

That night, sleep evaded me. I lay in the dark conjuring Margaret Clarke's face — though I had no idea what she actually looked like. I imagined elegant cheekbones, soft eyes hiding a tangle of secrets. What life had she lived? And more urgently — what had she known of Henry?

And then there was her son.

What did he know?

Morning arrived in a haze of weak sunlight and industrial-strength coffee. I was halfway through rearranging the biscuits for the fourth time when my phone rang. Unknown number.

I answered it, my stomach lurching. "Hello?"

A warm, calm voice came through. "Ms Whitman, good morning. This is David Tremayne from the First Evangelical Church in Quarry Hill. You emailed me yesterday."

"Yes!" I sat down, not trusting my legs. "Thank you for calling. I hope I haven't caught you at an inconvenient time?"

"Not at all," he said. "In fact, I wanted to speak with you before reaching out to Margaret's son. I thought it was only right, given your inquiry."

I nodded, even though he couldn't see me. "Of course. I appreciate that."

"Margaret passed away about four years ago. Quietly. Her health had been fading for some time. She was kind-hearted, but a private woman. I knew her more through our community meals than our services, to be honest."

A wave of disappointment settled over me. "I'm sorry to hear she passed. I'd hoped to speak with her... but yes, I understand."

"She had one child — a son, Robert Clinton Clarke. He still lives locally. Margaret never mentioned your name, which is why your advertisement caught my eye."

"I never knew her," I said quietly. "But I believe she may have known my husband, Henry Whitman. I'm piecing together parts of his life from before we met. Margaret might've been part of that past."

A pause.

Then David said gently, "Robert is... curious. Possibly wary. But not unkind." He's asked, "Why would seek out his mother now?"

I gave a short laugh. "That's fair. If someone placed an ad about my mother, I'd probably be suspicious too."

"I'll speak to him," David said. "If he's willing, he'll call you directly."

"Thank you," I said, trying not to sound as relieved as I felt.

Just as we wrapped up, I heard familiar voices outside. I peeked through the window and saw Shanice and Beatrice strolling up my path arm in arm, already mid-gossip. I stood quickly.

"The ladies are arriving," I told David. "We meet every Thursday. Coffee, cake, spirited opinions."

He chuckled. "Sounds lovely. I'll be in touch, Eleanor."

"Thank you again, David. Truly."

By the time I hung up, the house was full. Fiona had apparently brought her own corkscrew — because of course she had — and was already pouring rosé like it was Christmas Eve. She handed me a glass before I even made it to the kitchen.

Bethany arrived last, floating in with her trademark pale blue scarf and sunglasses, despite the thick cloud cover. She tossed her coat dramatically onto the rack as if she were stepping onto a Broadway stage.

"Oh, Eleanor, you've outdone yourself," she said, eyeing the dessert table. "Do you ever just serve a dry biscuit and call it a day?"

"Not while my self-worth is directly proportional to sponge height," I quipped.

The group burst into laughter and, just like that, we fell into our usual rhythm — stories, teasing, tangents, and wine refills.

But something in the air felt different. There was a restlessness beneath the surface. Bethany, usually the enigmatic one, was already on her third glass of rosé when she leant forward and announced, "Ladies — and Eleanor — I have a confession."

We paused, glasses frozen halfway to lips.

"I wasn't always the model citizen you see before you."

"Oh dear," Georgina muttered.

Bethany gave a smile that could only be described as feline. "When I was twenty-one, I was involved in an activist group. Thought we were noble. Turns out we were just dramatic, disillusioned, and tipsy most of the time."

"What kind of activist group?" asked Louisa, leaning in.

"Political. Fiercely leftist. We wanted to change the world. And maybe spray-paint it while we were at it."

"What did you do?" I asked.

"We planned a protest. It turned into a heist."

My eyebrows rose. "A heist?"

Bethany nodded, suddenly solemn. "We took documents. Government ones. Not for money — for the cause. But things went wrong. A guard nearly got hurt. We scattered. Some were caught. I wasn't. I changed my name. Got married. Taught third graders for thirty years."

Silence.

Then Diana piped up, "Did you just admit to an unsolved crime over wine and lemon tart?"

Bethany raised her glass. "Statute of limitations. I checked. Twice."

We howled with laughter. It echoed through the house like relief.

"Bethany, you taught my niece cursive!" Shanice said between gasps. "And you stole from the government?"

Bethany grinned. "With style, darling. With style."

The conversation unravelled into giggles and jabs, but my mind wandered. Secrets. So many of us lived with them. Carried them in our handbags like expired lipstick and loose receipts.

And then — my phone buzzed.

CHAPTER 16

An Ally

The phone rang mid-morning just as I was sliding the last of the plates into the dish drawer. My hand froze on the handle. A tightness curled low in my chest. Somehow, I already knew who it was.

I picked it up, doing my best to sound calm. "Hello?"

"Ms Whitman? This is Robert Clarke. David Tremayne said you wanted to speak with me about my mother?"

"Yes, thank you so much for calling," I said, pulling out a chair and easing myself into it. "I really appreciate it. I know this is probably out of the blue."

"That's alright." His voice was even, deliberate. He struck me instantly as someone who didn't waste breath. "David said you'd been asking about Margaret Clarke. I was curious."

"I understand," I said carefully. "I'm doing a bit of personal research. I came across your mother's name while looking through some old records. It's difficult to explain quickly, but I believe she may have had a connection to someone I'm researching."

There was a slight pause before he asked, "Connected how?"

There was something defensive in his tone, protective maybe. I couldn't blame him.

"I'm not entirely sure yet," I admitted. "But I came across a photograph of your mother, my late husband Henry Whitman, and another man. That third man. I don't know who he is. I thought perhaps he might've been a relative of hers. A brother maybe? Or a cousin?"

"Do you have a name for the third man?" he asked.

"No," I said. "Unfortunately, I don't. That's why I'm reaching out."

"Can you send me the photo? I might recognise him."

"Of course. Just give me a second. I'm hopeless when it comes to mobile technology." I let out a nervous laugh, fumbling for the photo I'd found at Willowmere. My fingers weren't entirely steady, but I managed to forward the image to his number.

There was a brief silence while he opened it.

Then he said, "I know the man. That's Thomas Harding."

My breath hitched. "You're certain?"

"Oh, that's him alright. That's Uncle Thomas. Same grin, same jacket. He always wore jackets like that. Mum must've been in her twenties here."

I hesitated. "You sound a little uncertain when you say, Uncle Thomas." "May I ask why?"

He let out a breath that might have passed for a laugh, but there was no humour in it. "Yeah. I was told to call him Uncle Tom my whole life. But as far as I ever knew, he wasn't actually related to us. Just always around."

I sat up straighter, instinct prickling.

"That's interesting. Because in all of Margaret's official records—her birth certificate, school files, census listings-she's always listed as an only child."

"That doesn't surprise me," Robert said flatly.

"He never talked much about his past. He'd show up every couple of weeks with a toolbox and a cheeky story. Fixed the taps, mowed the lawn, took Mum and me to the cinema, had too many beers on the back porch. He died about a year before Mum did."

"I'm sorry," I said gently.

I stared again at the photo, as if seeing it anew. Margaret standing beside Thomas Harding and Henry, all three smiling in that casual, timeless way people smile when they don't know they're leaving clues behind.

"So, if he wasn't really your uncle..." I began.

"He was my father," Robert said. Just like that. No hesitation.

My mouth went dry. "You're sure?"

"I've suspected for years," he said, his voice softer now. "But Mum never admitted it. She dodged the question every time. And Tom... he never said anything. They were close, but they never lived together. He'd stay a night or two and vanish for a week or more. Always like that."

"Do you think your mother kept the truth from you for a reason?"

"I do," he said after a pause. "I think she thought she was protecting me, or maybe herself. Tom had shadows, she'd say.

Never really fit in. Nice enough bloke, but distant. Like part of him wasn't there."

I swallowed.

"I think he may have been part of something bigger. Something connected to Henry." My voice wavered. "Have you ever heard of my husband, Henry Whitman?"

"No," he said. "Should I have?"

"Henry was a university professor and worked for the government. Someone's been calling my home and leaving cryptic messages. Then an anonymous envelope arrived with a photo, that photo, and that started all of this. If I'm right, Henry, and Thomas knew each other long before Margaret ever came into the picture."

"You think they were friends?"

"Maybe more. Colleagues. I don't know yet. I know nothing about Thomas Harding except what I've learned in scraps and half-memories."

Robert let out a low whistle. "That actually explains a few things."

"Such as?"

There was a pause. "I should probably tell you. I'm a homicide detective."

That caught me completely off guard.

"You're what?"

"Detective. Used to work in Sydney, transferred back here when Mum got sick. Twelve years on the job. I always told myself I didn't need to know more about Tom. That if he was decent to us, that was enough. But now..." He exhaled slowly. "Now I wonder if I was wilfully blind."

I felt something shift, like a door creaking open, just enough to catch a shaft of light. "Robert, if you're willing to look into this with me, maybe we can uncover what really happened. Who Thomas Harding was. What all of this means. Why your mother and my husband were connected. Why these secrets have survived all this time."

"You think it's all connected?"

"I do," I said, my voice steady. "I found another photo, just of Henry and Thomas. They're standing outside a CBA bank branch. The windows were shuttered closed after a robbery decades ago. I think whatever they were part of changed them. Changed Margaret. And you."

He didn't speak for a moment.

Then: "Alright. I'll do it. I'll dig into Tom Harding. Pull up whatever I can. Cross-reference the archives. Maybe something will pop."

"I'll send you everything I have," I offered. "Photos, letters, records. Maybe you'll notice something I didn't."

"I'll start with a national database search. Criminal records. Government connections. You never know."

There was a pause.

Then he asked almost quietly, "Do you think my mum knew everything about him?"

I thought about Margaret's face in that photograph—how her smile reached her eyes but didn't erase the wariness beneath.

"I think she knew enough," I said. "Enough to be afraid. And enough to protect you."

He let out a sharp exhale. "Then maybe it's time I stop letting her protect me."

"Yes," I said softly. "Maybe it is."

We ended the call with promises to stay in touch, to share everything we found. For the first time in weeks, I felt something stir. Not quite hope—but momentum.

I stood at the kitchen window, coffee cup in hand, watching the breeze scatter petals across the garden. Somewhere, behind all the sealed records and unfinished stories, the truth was waiting.

And I had a feeling that with Robert Clarke on my side, Detective Clarke, we might just be able to find it.

CHAPTER 17

Fragments and Fiction

After I hung up with Robert Clarke, I sat there for a long while, the receiver still warm in my hand. The silence in the kitchen wasn't peaceful—it was full and humming, like something unseen was charging the air. I stared out the window, where late-morning sunlight made lazy patterns on the tiled floor.

Detective Robert Clinton Clarke.

It still didn't feel real.

It was as if I'd stumbled into one of those old noir novels I devoured as a teenager—only this one had fewer trench coats and far more encrypted emails. A homicide detective. A son raised on half-truths. A man who had vanished like smoke from a bonfire, leaving only stories and questions in his wake. And now, that man's son—a reluctant detective in more ways than one—had agreed to look into the ruins of his own history.

I should've felt elated. Finally, a new lead. A new partner in this strange pursuit. But all I could think about was Margaret.

Margaret Clarke. With her sharp eyes and that gentle smile in the photograph. A smile that said she knew things— things she'd carried quietly for decades. What was it like, I wondered, to raise a child and never tell him the truth about his father? To let Thomas Harding hover on the fringes of their lives—always present but never permanent?

Was it protection? Fear? A consequence of something much larger—something shaped by the shadow Henry left behind?

The pattern kept changing. Each new revelation rearranged everything that came before it. And now, I had a detective on my side—a man with access, insight and, perhaps most importantly, motivation.

But I couldn't just sit around waiting for him to get back to me. That's never been my way. I got up and paced to the window, arms folded tight across my chest. The jacaranda in the front yard swayed gently in the breeze, its leaves scattering to the ground like memories shaken loose.

The truth was that the call had unsettled me more than I expected. Not just because of what I'd learned—but because I felt something shift. This wasn't a solitary quest anymore. It involved people now. People with lives and wounds, people who hadn't asked to be drawn into my search.

Robert had courage. I admired that. It takes a kind of personal bravery to look at the people who raised you and ask, "What were you hiding?"

It made me think of my mother. My own silences.

A soft knock pulled me out of my thoughts. The post. I peeked through the glass and saw the courier stepping off the porch. I opened the door, murmured a thank-you, and took the padded envelope. A book I'd ordered: The Archivist's Shadow.

Well. That felt... appropriate.

I left it unopened on the hallway table. My mind was still thick with thoughts of Thomas Harding and Margaret and the black-and-white photo that had somehow turned into a doorway.

I needed a different kind of escape. Not the kind that required a suitcase—but the kind that only writers know. I climbed the stairs to my study.

My little sanctuary.

The smell of paper, dust, and something just a little sweet greeted me. The sunlight filtered in through gauzy curtains and painted rippling shapes across my desk. On the far wall, my corkboard sagged under the weight of notes, clippings, character sketches—some thoughtful, others absurd.

One caught my eye: "What would Mildred do if she found a gun in the compost heap?" I grinned. That one had definitely come from a wine-fuelled Thursday night.

I sat at the desk and opened my laptop. The screen flickered to life, and the blinking cursor greeted me like a familiar dare.

I opened the file: The Latte Ladies – Draft 1.

Even the title made me smile.

What had started as a light-hearted project had grown teeth—and charm—and opinions of its own. A group of women who met every Thursday, originally at a café, now rotating between their homes. Each of them was wrapped in her own mystery. Her own story.

And one—of course—with a past that refused to stay buried.

I skimmed the outline.

Jean thinks the new barista might be her long-lost nephew (but he's too handsome to be related, surely?).

Doris confesses she once smuggled a llama across state lines during what she called her "spiritually open years."

And Mildred—bless her—keeps a notebook to log everyone's "suspicious behaviour", only to discover she's secretly a brilliant crime writer.

It was mad. Warm. Utterly ridiculous. And I loved it.

But as I stared at the document, a new idea surfaced. One of the Latte Ladies could have a Thomas Harding of her own— a man from the past who reappears unexpectedly through a photo or a call. Someone who meant more than anyone ever knew.

Yes.

Yes, that could work.

I opened a new page and typed:

Chapter Twelve – The Ghost with Grease on His Hands

And just like that, I was writing again.

Not to run away from the truth—but to reach toward it. To process it. To follow its scent like a bloodhound through fiction and fact alike.

Because sometimes, writing isn't about escaping life.

Sometimes, it's how we survive it.

CHAPTER 18

A Silly Game

By the time I arrived at Naomi's house, I was already fraying at the edges. That particular kind of emotional weariness that comes from stirring too many secrets and settling none of them. Her little house—with its squeaky garden gate, overgrown lavender that always brushed against my shins, and a doorbell that sounded like a kazoo gasping for breath—was already alive with chatter and bursts of laughter. Beautiful chaos. Familiar, welcome chaos. The kind that wraps itself around you like a hand-knitted scarf, a little scratchy but warm.

Naomi opened the door with a steaming mug of tea in one hand and a red feather boa draped across her shoulders like it was a silk shawl from the Moulin Rouge. "You're late," she said, her eyes twinkling. "Which means you're right on time."

"Is everyone here already?"

"Everyone but Vivian. She emailed me, saying she couldn't make it tonight."

Something about that tugged at me, though I tried not to show it. I followed Naomi down her narrow hallway, carefully stepping over a pile of books, a collection of mismatched shoes and what may have once been a cat bed—or perhaps a collapsed hatbox. We reached the kitchen, where the others had already settled into their familiar rhythm: Bethany with her ever-present rosé, Shanice fussing with a fruit platter no one would eat, and Fiona muttering about the lack of gluten-free options while sneakily chewing a shortbread biscuit.

Midyear always brought something of a reckoning to our group. The high of New Year's resolutions had long since faded. Dreams were being delayed, health issues hinted at, marriages looked a bit rumpled around the edges. We were all somewhere between holding it together and letting it all go—with just enough optimism to keep showing up.

Naomi's solution? "Truth or Dare."

"This is childish," Zoe muttered, clinging to her wineglass like a flotation device.

"Exactly," Naomi chirped, tossing a velvet hat onto the table. "Sometimes childish is exactly what we need to be honest."

Bethany reached into the hat first. "Truth," she said quickly, likely fearing we'd dare her to perform burlesque on Naomi's wobbly coffee table.

Naomi pulled a folded slip and read aloud: "If you could go back and change one decision, what would it be?"

Silence.

Bethany stared into her glass. "I would've stayed in New Zealand. There was someone I left behind. Thought I could forget them. I was wrong. I was young. A political activist without a clue."

No one said anything. No one had to. The silence itself was reverent.

Then Zoe, emboldened now, pulled a slip. "Dare."

Naomi's grin could have lit a small village. "Call your husband. Tell him you forgive her."

Zoe's smile vanished. "That's low, Naomi."

"It's real," Naomi said, unapologetic.

"I won't do it," Zoe said, lifting her phone anyway. "But if I did, I'd put it on speaker, so we all suffer together."

That set the tone. Little truths. Big ones. Wounds we'd hidden under layers of polite conversation spilled out, staining the tablecloth like red wine on white linen. It was wild, absurd—and strangely beautiful.

Then it was my turn.

"Truth," I said, barely above a whisper. I couldn't bear the thought of a dare.

Naomi reached into the hat, pulled a card, and read: "What's the biggest thing you've told no one?"

The words hung in the air, expectant. My throat felt dry. My hands shook slightly.

"I once gave someone up," I said. "A long time ago. And I've never stopped thinking about them."

The silence that followed wasn't judgemental. It was gentle. Solid. Like a hand resting on your back, letting you know you weren't alone.

That's what I loved about them. These women. We didn't pry. We didn't fix. We simply held space—for grief, for confession, for banana bread and rosé.

By the time I slipped away from Naomi's house, the stars were winking above the rooftops and my heart felt fuller. Heavier, yes—but somehow clearer.

Back home, I kicked off my shoes and poured a small glass of sherry. I told myself I was only going to check emails. Maybe jot down a line or two. Nothing major.

But as I settled at my desk, my eyes drifted to the bottom drawer.

The one I hadn't opened in years.

Before I could talk myself out of it, I reached for it.

Inside was the envelope.

Letters. Notes. Hospital documents. And one photo.

Just one.

A newborn wrapped in a faded blue blanket turned slightly toward the light. Her eyes were closed; her features were impossibly delicate.

My daughter.

I hadn't allowed myself to look at that photo in so long. Now, I traced its edge with my fingertip, as if I could somehow touch her through time. She'd be in her late twenties now. Perhaps with children of her own. Perhaps with my chin or my laugh—or Henry's stubborn quietude.

And all this time, I had been a ghost. Hovering outside her life.

Was it Vivian?

I didn't know. I had only questions. And guilt. And the aching sense that time is both a thief and a strange kind of mercy.

I turned back to the laptop. The Latte Ladies document was still open, the cursor blinking like a pulse.

I began typing:

Chapter Fourteen – The One That Got Away

Edith never spoke about her daughter. The one she gave up before her nineteenth birthday. The one whose name she never knew. But on a Thursday morning, over banana bread and tears, she finally whispered the story that had haunted her for forty years...

I wrote until the screen blurred. Until the ache in my chest loosened. Until I felt something shift—not just in the story, but in me.

When I finished the chapter, I saved the file and attached it to a new e-mail.

Subject: Something new...
To: Vivian Mendez
Body:
Hi Vivian,
I've been working on a new chapter and thought you might have some thoughts. It's rough, but I'd love your feedback, especially on the new character.
Let me know if you have time.
Warmly,
Eleanor

I clicked send and just like that, a small part of my heart—quiet and trembling—flew through the ether to Vivian. Not just as a reader.

But maybe, just maybe, as a daughter.

CHAPTER 19

Zoe's Decision

Zoe pulled into her driveway just after ten, the wheels of her car crunching over the gravel, announcing her arrival. She sat in the car for a while, the engine off, her fingers still curled around the steering wheel. Naomi's dare echoed through her head like an unfinished sentence.

"I dare you to call him. Tonight."

Zoe had laughed it off.

Deflected with a joke about needing more wine before facing that kind of emotional warfare. But now, in the quiet shell of her parked car, the dare didn't feel playful. It felt prophetic.

She stepped inside her townhouse and locked the door behind her with more intention than usual. The house was still, save for the hum of the refrigerator and the occasional creak of timber that always made her imagine ghosts she wasn't afraid of. She dropped her bag by the hallway table and walked straight to the kitchen, where she poured herself a glass of water and leant against the counter.

Call him?

What would she say? What would he say?

She could already hear his voice.

Measured, patronising, well-practised: "You're being paranoid again, Zoe. You're reading too much into things. It's late. I have an important meeting. Go to bed. I will see you on the weekend." Or worse, the newer tone he'd adopted lately.

Softly, falsely, sympathetically: "You've been under a lot of stress. Let's talk when you're feeling more balanced."

The bastard. He was probably in bed with her now, *"... getting ready for his morning meeting."*

She would not give him that opening again.

Zoe exhaled slowly and made her way upstairs. In the second drawer of her bedside table, beneath a pile of bank statements and expired cosmetics, sat a leather-bound folder. She pulled it out with careful hands, as though it might shatter in her grip.

Inside were her notes along with the evidence she had gathered after she had seen him with the other 'wife' and son.

Screenshots.

Emails.

Jewellery invoices.

The damned voice message from a number she'd once assumed was work-related until she'd heard a giggle and her husband's unmistakable voice say, "I can't wait to see you again, kitten."

The folder was damning.

But more than that, it was heavy.

Emotionally. Psychologically. Professionally.

Zoe sank onto the edge of the bed and ran her hand over the cover. A divorce meant more than just the end of a marriage.

It meant press, scrutiny, gossip.

She wasn't just a woman in crisis.

She was a high-powered corporate attorney with bosses and clients who cared about image and optics. If this blew up, it could tarnish not just his reputation, but hers too. There was no escaping the irony: the woman who spun disasters for a living had quietly been living one for the past years.

Wasn't this why she had stayed silent so long?

To protect a name she didn't want anymore.

She looked around the bedroom.

Spotless, neutral, curated, empty of love.

A room made for appearances.

A life lived in well-staged corners.

No more.

Zoe stood, placed the folder into her briefcase, and zipped it shut.

She didn't need to call him. Not tonight. Never, perhaps.

What she needed now was a lawyer.

A professional who wouldn't care how charming her husband was, or how pretty his lies sounded. Someone who would see the truth for what it was and help her carve a way out.

She opened her laptop and began researching divorce attorneys. By midnight, she had three consultations booked for the next day.

It wasn't a confrontation. It was action.

That thought brought her strange comfort.

Still, as she lay in bed staring at the ceiling, a wave of doubt crept in.

The fear didn't come from the divorce itself; it came from what came after.

The headlines.

The whispers.

The way people in their world would phrase it: "Such a shame, really. They seemed so perfect."

Would her clients stay?

Would they question her judgement?

Would they think her weak for not seeing it sooner?

And worse still, what would the ladies of the coffee group think?

The women had shared so much tonight.

Secrets. Regrets. Wounds they didn't speak about in polite company.

Naomi's unresolved grief.

Bethany's past in New Zealand.

Eleanor's confession about giving someone up.

Was it time?

Yes. It was.

Zoe reached for her phone and typed a message into the group chat but didn't send it.

She saved the message and set the phone down, her eyes closing slowly. Tomorrow would come fast. There'd be questions. Legalese. Paperwork. Maybe tears. But there would also be something else.

Freedom.

Zoe wasn't calling him.

She was calling her own bluff.

And finally, she was ready to win.

CHAPTER 20

Naomi Confronted

By the time I stood in Naomi's kitchen, the last of the mugs and wine glasses were drying upside down on the rack. It had been a good evening. Chaotic, cathartic, beautiful in the way that only a night of slightly tipsy truth-telling among friends could be. There'd been laughter, yes, but also long silences, hard confessions, and a kind of quiet healing that tiptoed in when no one was looking.

The house had fallen still again.

It was Naomi's space once more.

Her sanctuary.

She'd shed the red feather boa an hour earlier and traded her hostess grin for pyjamas and a messy bun. We'd hugged at the door, murmured our goodbyes. I remember thinking she looked lighter, exhausted but unburdened, like the night had wrung something out of her.

Then, just as she reached for the kitchen light, her phone buzzed on the counter.

Once.

Twice.

The screen lit up with a name she hadn't expected to see.

Michael Harper.

She told me later that she'd saved his name once, a long time ago, when she was still tangled in anonymous payments and quiet penance, but she never imagined he'd use it.

She didn't answer.

She couldn't.

Not that night, when her heart was still sore from a dozen shared secrets and her hands still smelt of lavender dish soap.

The ringing stopped.

A pause.

Then the soft chime of a voicemail.

She didn't want to hear it.

But of course, she did.

She leant against the sink and pressed play.

"Naomi, it's Michael. I know it's you. The anonymous payments. The flowers. The notes with no name. It was you all along. I don't know what to say, but I need to speak with you. In person. I'm coming to your office tomorrow morning, and I want answers about my wife. About you. About why? I deserve that."

She sat down hard at the kitchen table, her knees suddenly unreliable. The words kept playing in her mind long after the message ended. That voice was gravelled, stunned, but calm. Not angry. Not yet.

She told me later she'd always known this moment might come. She just hadn't expected it to arrive on the heels of rosé and banana bread when her emotional walls were still soaked through.

Michael Harper.

The man whose grief she'd haunted for a year.

The widower of the woman she hadn't saved.

The morning came too quickly. She barely slept. She walked into the hospital cloaked in a kind of grey — the sky, her mood, her certainty. Every version of the conversation played out in her mind, each one more difficult than the last. None of them ended well.

He was already there.

Tall, still, hands shoved into his jacket pockets like they were holding him up. His hair had silvered more since the funeral, but his eyes were the same: tired, searching, wounded.

"Naomi," he said.

She nodded. "Michael. Let's find a quiet place."

They walked in silence down the hallway, and when they reached a small meeting room, she gestured for him to enter. Closed the door behind them. Rested her hand on the cold metal knob a second too long.

He didn't sit. Just stood by the window, staring out.

"It was you," he said.

She nodded. "Yes. All this time."

"The money. The flowers. The birthday cards with no name. The cemetery visits."

"Yes," she whispered. "It was me."

"Why?"

The word wasn't bitter. Just hollow. Spent.

She swallowed hard. "Because I couldn't keep pretending that it didn't matter. That her death didn't matter."

"You mean Olivia?"

Naomi flinched. "Yes. I wasn't supposed to leave her side, but I did. Just for a minute. And something shifted in that minute. Something I missed. It was fast. Too fast. The internal review cleared me of fault, but I couldn't shake it. I still can't."

She said her guilt had been a weight she carried in silence. That the acts of kindness, the flowers, the payments, even the birthday gestures, weren't attempts at redemption. They were the only way she knew how to stay connected to the woman she couldn't save.

Michael turned toward her. Something in him softened, just barely.

"I was going to yell at you today," he said. "Maybe even threaten a lawsuit. I rehearsed it in the car."

She looked at him, eyes rimmed red. "And now?"

He was quiet. Then, "Now, I think I needed to see you. To hear it. Not just for answers, but to stop chasing a ghost I didn't know I was chasing."

She told me later that the relief she felt in that moment wasn't relief at being absolved. She didn't think she ever would be. But it was the relief of being seen, even in her guilt. Especially in it.

"I'm not asking you to forgive me," she said. "I just needed to stop hiding."

Michael sat then, slowly. And for a few minutes, they sat together, not doctor and widower, not accuser and accused — but two people joined by the same grief, just from different angles.

"You sent flowers on the day she died," he said.

Naomi nodded, her voice barely above a whisper. "Every year."

"You paid for Eli's counselling."

She nodded again. "I needed him to have something I couldn't give her. A second chance. A safety net."

He let out a slow exhale. "I don't know if I can be okay with it. But I'm glad I know. And I'm glad you didn't run."

Neither of them had expected peace that day. But something else bloomed between them — acknowledgment, perhaps. The truth lay bare.

And sometimes, that's where healing begins. Not with forgiveness. But with the willingness to sit in the same room and not look away.

CHAPTER 21

Vivian's Moment of Truth

I'd just arranged a fresh plate of almond biscuits when I noticed Vivian standing by the hallway mirror, smoothing her blouse for the third time. She wasn't fidgety by nature. Vivian always carried herself with a kind of quiet focus, but today, there was something different. Her hands moved with too much precision, like she was trying to silence the tremor beneath them.

I'd invited some of the ladies for a quiet Saturday afternoon — a smaller gathering than usual. Zoe had offered to bring a bottle of wine, claiming she needed "less drama and more grenache" after the week she'd had. Naomi was on shift, and Bethany was visiting her niece, the other ladies busy, so it was just the three of us, and I had expected the mood to be easier somehow. But I could sense the storm sitting just off the horizon of Vivian's expression.

She was waiting for a moment.

I didn't know what, or why, but I could feel it pressing against the edges of the room like humidity before a thunderclap.

Zoe arrived ten minutes later, her heels clicking across the timber floor, a scarf tossed casually over one shoulder.

"Ladies," she called, holding the wine like a trophy, "I come bearing libations and zero emotional baggage. Who's thirsty?"

Vivian managed a smile, but I noticed how she gripped the stem of her glass a little too tightly when I poured. She barely sipped.

We sat in the lounge, the late afternoon light softening the corners of the room. I asked Zoe about her meetings with the lawyers, and she shared just enough to update us, but not enough to break the mood. She seemed more settled than I'd seen her in weeks, which only made Vivian's silence more pronounced.

I watched her.

The way her gaze kept flicking from me to the small satchel beside her on the floor. She hadn't let it out of her reach since she had arrived. I'd bet money that inside was whatever she'd been quietly investigating these past few months.

I could feel her preparing.

Bracing.

And I waited, unsure if I wanted the reveal or dreaded it.

But then, Zoe turned to her with that unnervingly perceptive glance of hers and said, "Vivian, are you okay? You've been quieter than usual, and I know for a fact you're not afraid of Eleanor's almond biscuits."

Vivian laughed too quickly, too loudly, and then shook her head. "I'm fine. Just tired."

Zoe didn't blink.

She shifted forward, resting her wineglass on her knee, and lowered her voice. "Look, I'm no psychic, but I know the face of someone holding back something big. Believe me, I invented it."

There was a beat of silence.

Vivian looked down at her hands.

"I brought something today," she said. "I thought I'd... I don't know. I thought I'd be ready to talk about it."

I felt my breath still.

Something fluttered inside me.

Instinct?

Guilt?

Hope?

She reached for her satchel but didn't open it.

Her fingers just hovered over the zipper.

"I've been doing some personal research," she continued. "Trying to understand more about my past."

Zoe didn't press.

Just waited, her posture calm and open.

Vivian looked over at me, and our eyes met.

There it was so raw, so familiar. That tightrope walk between curiosity and fear. She was trying to decide whether I was the ground or the chasm.

I tried to hold her gaze without flinching.

"Take your time," I said gently. "You don't owe us anything you're not ready to share."

Vivian exhaled slowly, then turned to Zoe.

"Do you ever worry that the truth might just make everything worse?"

Zoe raised an eyebrow.

"All the damn time. But I've also learned that carrying secrets is like carrying wet sand. You think it'll dry out if you hold it long enough, but it just gets heavier."

Vivian smiled faintly. "That's an excellent metaphor."

"It's not mine. Eleanor said it once when I was neck-deep in denial," Zoe said, throwing me a wink. "She's full of those annoying truths."

I gave a soft chuckle and shrugged.

"Occupational hazard of being old and nosy."

That broke the tension.

Vivian laughed too, this time for real.

Then she tucked the satchel to her side and said, "Not today. But soon."

Zoe nodded. "We'll be here."

And I saw something shift between them.

A quiet pact. Zoe, who had just learned how to let go, was somehow lending Vivian the space to hold on a little longer.

I brought out the biscuits. We refilled glasses.

The afternoon wore on in that gentle way some afternoons do, unresolved but softened.

There would be another day.

Another conversation.

But when Vivian hugged me goodbye, she held on just a second longer than usual.

And I felt it in my bones: the moment is coming.

Whatever it is she's found, it will change everything.

And this time, I'll be ready.

CHAPTER 22

George's Announcement

I'd just taken the blueberry tart out of the oven when the doorbell rang. The house already smelled of butter, sugar, and cinnamon - the sort of scent that makes even secrets feel a little safer.

Bethany arrived first, in a cloud of Chanel No. 5 and opinions about parking enforcement. Then Zoe breezed in with a bottle of prosecco and a bag of fancy olives "no one asked for, but everyone will eat." Naomi showed up not long after, hair still damp from her morning swim, cheeks flushed with that post-exercise glow I've never been able to relate to.

Fiona, Natalie, and Shanice strolled in together, all giddy-like.

Georgina — George, as she insisted we call her — was last. She hovered at the doorway longer than usual, like she wasn't quite ready to cross the threshold.

"You alright, love?" I asked.

She gave a bright smile that didn't quite reach her eyes. "Yep. All good. Just got caught in my head for a second."

She handed me a brown paper bag with two loaves of rye sourdough, still warm. "Bribery," she said. "For letting me eat three servings of your quiche last time."

I waved her in, and we settled into the lounge with cups of tea and slices of tart that barely had time to cool. The group was in good spirits, more relaxed than we'd been in weeks.

Maybe it was the weather, spring finally teasing its way back through the windows, or maybe we were all just a little lighter after our last gathering, where half the room had bared their souls between sips of wine and forkfuls of banana bread.

When the laughter lulled and the conversation thinned, I noticed George shifting in her seat. She wasn't her usual self.

No dry quips, no raised-eyebrow commentary about Fiona's conspiracy theories or Bethany's fondness for the royal family.

She was quiet.

Careful.

I was about to nudge her gently with a benign question about sourdough hydration when she cleared her throat.

"Can I say something?"

The room went still.

Zoe glanced up from her glass.

Naomi stopped slicing cheese.

Bethany set her rosé down with an audible clink.

And Fiona, Natalie, and Shanice just stared.

"Of course," I said, trying to keep my voice casual.

George sat forward, palms flat on her knees.

"I wasn't sure if I'd say anything today. Or ever, really. But I think maybe I've been waiting for the right people to say it to."

No one moved.

Not even Bethany, which told me everything I needed to know.

George took a breath. "I'm gay."

The words hung there for a moment, not heavy, but electric.

Real.

Beautifully unadorned.

She looked up, bracing herself for what, exactly, I wasn't sure.

Judgement?

Silence?

The kind of awkwardness that clings to you long after everyone's gone home.

But it didn't come.

Naomi, bless her, simply said, "Okay," and reached for another cracker like George had just announced she'd repainted her hallway.

Bethany blinked and then, to everyone's surprise, said, "So was my cousin Margaret. Tough as nails. She could drink any bloke under the table and still get up and do the church flowers the next morning."

Zoe raised her glass. "I always knew I liked you for a reason, George."

Fiona, Natalie, and Shanice just nodded, with Fiona saying simply: "Good on ya!"

George laughed, but I saw the way her shoulders dropped just slightly, the way her grip on the cushion beside her loosened. The tension she'd walked in with was melting.

"There's more," she said, still smiling, but now with the confidence that comes from the truth no longer being locked behind your teeth. "I'm opening a bakery."

That made everyone lean forward.

"In Picton," she continued. "It's - well, it's not just mine. I'm doing it with my brother. He was discharged last month. PTSD. He's been adrift ever since, and I figured if we're going to start something, it might as well be something warm. Something that smells like bread. Something kind."

There was a silence, not awkward, but reverent.

And then Naomi said, "That's one of the best ideas I've heard in ages."

Zoe nodded.

"What do you need? Investors? Taste-testers? Publicity? Because I have no shame in writing a glowing review before the first croissant is even baked."

"I don't know yet," George said, eyes glassy now.

"I just know I want it to be more than a bakery. I want it to be a place people can breathe. Especially people who've forgotten how."

"You'll make it that," I said softly. "You already make this group feel that way."

Her eyes met mine, and something passed between us then — something quiet and whole.

A recognition.

A gratitude.

I felt my throat tighten.

"Thank you," she said.

We sat with her story for a while.

Asked questions about the building she'd found, the oven she wanted to install, her brother's surprising skill with short crust pastry.

Naomi volunteered to help design a mental health-friendly workspace.

Zoe offered to draw up a marketing plan.

Bethany said she'd donate antique cake stands if George promised not to put those trendy little cupcakes with edible glitter on them.

And I offered to help her write the welcome letter for the shop window. Because that's what I do. I write. And sometimes, when I'm lucky, my words land where they're needed.

Later, when everyone had gone and the last crumb had been wiped from the plates, I stared at the kettle, thinking of George and her brother and the quiet power of being seen.

Coming out.

Starting over.

Building something out of kindness, flour, and grief.

It reminded me gently that the stories we tell when we're ready to tell them have the power to stitch people together in ways we never expect.

And that, perhaps, was the very heart of our group.

Not the tea. Not the tart.

But the truth.

And how we hold each other in it.

I did smile as I went into the kitchen at George's announcement, because we always knew - and we did not care.

CHAPTER 23

Diana in Flight

I was at Beatrice Torre's home helping Beatrice get the house ready for our next get-together, when the kettle had just begun its gentle rattle and I heard the commotion outside Beatrice's front door. It wasn't the usual knock or chatter of arrivals — it was something quieter, but urgent. Like a whisper with weight.

I looked for Beatrice, but she was upstairs changing, so I stood near the hallway, teacup in hand, watching through the etched glass as a shape moved near the porch. A figure bent low, as if placing something deliberately at the doorstep.

Vivian got there first.

She'd gone out moments earlier to take a phone call, pacing along the garden path with that furrowed brow of hers that always made me think she was solving the world's mysteries one step at a time. But now, she was standing still, facing Diana — our Diana, our Di — who looked more like a startled bird than the vibrant woman we all knew. Her eyes were rimmed with exhaustion, shoulders hunched under the weight of a worn backpack, and her hand was still frozen mid-drop over a sealed envelope with our group's name written in her graceful, looping hand.

"Di?" Vivian said gently, stepping closer. "What are you doing?"

Di flinched. "Nothing, I... God. I didn't want... I didn't think anyone would be here so early."

Vivian reached out, resting a hand on her arm. "Why would you leave a letter on the doorstep?"

Di looked at her, and for a moment I saw the walls collapse. She didn't speak, just shook her head — small, trembling motions that said more than words could.

"Come inside," Vivian whispered. "Please. Come inside."

I had already opened the door before Di could argue.

The others were gathered in the lounge.

Zoe rearranging cushions, Bethany organising biscuits by size (her version of meditative order), Naomi swiping through her phone. Beatrice had just come downstairs. The moment they saw Vivian guiding Di in, everything stopped.

Di's face was pale, eyes glassy, her whole body carrying the weight of something unspoken.

"I was just going to leave the letter," she said finally. "I didn't want to make a scene."

Vivian closed the door behind her. "Then let's make a safe one."

That's when I stepped forward, still holding my teacup, as if a bit of china could anchor the world.

"Darling girl," I said softly, "you don't have to run. Not from us."

Di blinked, startled. "But I have told no one. Not even my partner. I've been hiding it. For months."

"Then you must be so tired," I said. "And I don't just mean the kind of tired sleep fixes."

She nodded with a brittle motion. Her hands gripped the straps of her backpack as if they were the only things holding her together.

"It's a chronic condition," she said. "An autoimmune thing. Fatigue, pain, nausea. Some days I can't even get out of bed. And I've been pretending. At home, with Marcus, with all of you. But it's getting worse. And I thought — maybe if I left quietly, no one would be burdened. No one would have to... look at me differently."

"Oh, Di," Naomi murmured.

"I didn't want pity," Di said, voice cracking. "And I didn't want to break the way we are. The laughter. The silliness. I didn't want to be the reason everything changed."

I set my cup down and crossed the room, stopping just in front of her. "We don't love you because you're strong. Or cheerful. Or high functioning. We love you because you're ours. Just as we are yours."

She sobbed then — loud and unguarded — and I took her hand.

"Listen to me," I said, voice steady. "We all walk through fire in our own ways. And sometimes we carry buckets of water for each other. You don't get to decide whether you're worthy of that. You already are. You don't need to hide your pain to be loved. You already are."

Vivian handed her a tissue, Zoe wrapped an arm around her shoulder, and Bethany — bless her — just cried quietly, whispering something about her sister who'd suffered in silence too.

We all cried then. The whole bloody room.

It wasn't dramatic.

It wasn't performative.

It was real.

Raw, messy, honest.

After a few minutes, Di pulled the letter from her pocket and tore it in half. "I guess I won't be needing this."

"You'll need something else instead," I said, smiling through my tears. "Help. Patience. Someone to bring you soup on the rough days. Someone to remind you that you're still whole, even when your body isn't behaving."

Naomi chimed in, "And someone to watch terrible Netflix series with you and say wildly inappropriate things to make you laugh."

"And banana bread," Bethany added solemnly. "Always banana bread."

Di laughed through a sob and nodded. "You lot are impossible."

"Absolutely," I said. "And absolutely yours."

We spent the rest of the afternoon on the floor, with cushions and blankets and warm mugs, Di curled between us like someone returning to a nest she hadn't realised she'd built with her own hands.

She wasn't leaving anymore.

And none of us would ever let her feel like she had to.

CHAPTER 24

Revelations

The cushions were still warm from where Diana had sat, huddled in the centre of us all like a bird caught in a storm. We lingered around her; the kettle refilled twice; tissues passed from hand to hand like communion. The house smelled of mint tea, banana bread, and the salty tang of tears.

I was still sitting cross-legged on the floor, the hem of my linen trousers wrinkled and damp from an earlier spill. Diana, now wrapped in my old cardigan, looked pale but steadier. Her hands were no longer clenched. Her voice no longer trembled. Her decision to stay had already transformed her face. The shadow of departure had lifted.

"You know," I said gently, "I think today might be the most honest this group has ever been."

"Speak for yourself," Naomi muttered with a small smile, wiping her nose. "I've been waiting years to hear Beatrice admit she's human."

A nervous giggle stirred through the group.

Then Beatrice, our Beatrice, the flamboyant, bendy-limbed yoga queen in her eternally colourful tights and chakra earrings, suddenly sniffled.

Loudly.

We all turned.

Beatrice didn't cry.

Beatrice made other people cry, usually with laughter.

But now she was blinking hard and shaking her head like a woman betrayed by her own tear ducts.

"Oh, love," I whispered, reaching for her hand. "What is it?"

She waved me off, sniffling again, clearly trying to compose herself.

"It's stupid. Honestly. I shouldn't have, but seeing Di like that, and all of us, it just got to me."

"Nothing's stupid when your face looks like it just survived a soap opera," Naomi said, scooting closer.

Beatrice laughed, an odd, strangled sound, and looked down at her lap.

"I'm in love with someone I absolutely shouldn't be."

A pause.

"Oh no," whispered Zoe. "It's George Clooney, isn't it? You swore you were over him."

We all chuckled nervously.

Beatrice didn't.

"It's my best friend's husband," she said.

Dead silence.

My hand dropped from hers in surprise, then returned just as quickly.

Bethany's wine glass was halfway to her mouth. She lowered it slowly.

"I think he might feel the same," Beatrice added, voice barely above a whisper.

"We've never acted on it. Never even spoken of it directly. But there's something. The way he looks at me when she's not watching. The way I feel when he's near me. It's like gravity. And I hate myself for it."

For a long moment, no one said anything.

The outside world felt impossibly far away.

I cleared my throat. "Have you ever told anyone?"

She shook her head.

"Not even him?"

"No, especially not him. I couldn't do that to her. She's been my best friend since high school."

Zoe, who had remained oddly still, suddenly stood up and walked to the bookshelf. Her back was to us. She touched the spine of a novel and stared at it as if it might contain instructions for what to say next.

"We can't control who we fall for," Naomi said softly now, all jokes set aside. "But we can control what we do with it."

Beatrice nodded.

"I know. I haven't done anything. I never will. I just needed to say it somewhere. Aloud. To someone."

"You said it to the right people," I said. "There's nothing we haven't survived in this room. Heartache included."

"Speaking of which," Zoe said suddenly, turning around. Her voice had changed — tight, brittle.

We all looked up.

"I haven't told you all, not properly. I told Naomi after a dare, and I think Eleanor knows more than she lets on, but I'm filing for divorce."

Gasps. Naomi covered her mouth. Diana looked stricken.

"He has another family," Zoe added flatly. "A woman. A child. A whole double life. And I knew. For months. I didn't want to believe it. But now it's real. I've booked appointments. I've got a folder full of evidence in my bag right now."

"Oh, Zoe," I whispered, standing slowly.

She raised a hand, silencing any sympathy.

"I don't want pity. I want the truth. Like what we've all been sharing. So, there it is. I'm done hiding."

There was a murmur of agreement.

Heads nodding.

Then Bethany cleared her throat.

"I should probably say something too," she said, suddenly shy. "My son - he's in prison. Fraud charges. And I've been telling everyone he's overseas teaching English."

Silence again.

Bethany, the meticulous widow, always proper, always measured, looked so small as she said it. I reached for her hand across the rug.

"You're still the mother who bakes the best scones in Northport, NSW," I said. "And we love you just the same."

"I haven't spoken to him in over a year," she admitted. "But I think I want to. I think I need to."

Vivian, who had been quiet throughout, finally spoke.

"I have something too. I think I might know who my birth mother is. I've been researching. Following clues. And I think it's someone we all know."

Every cell in my body stood still.

My throat tightened.

I knew what she was trying to say.

Or rather, not say.

Yet.

But she didn't meet my eyes.

"I haven't said anything because I'm not sure yet. Not really. But it's been on my mind constantly. I can't sleep. I can't work. I have not done a photography shoot in weeks. Every time I look around this group, I wonder if any of you have guessed."

Naomi let out a breath. "Well, now I'm going to lose sleep, too."

Vivian offered a half-smile.

Beatrice touched her arm. "When you're ready, we'll be here. All of us."

Vivian nodded.

The room swelled with something holy in that moment.

The air thick with honesty and things we'd carried alone far too long.

Naomi stood and raised her mug. "To us, broken things. To secrets. To truth. To banana bread."

We all laughed and raised whatever we had — tea, wine, tissues.

And I said, "To this group. The wild, honest mess of us. May we never run from each other again."

There were more tears then, and more laughter.

Someone turned on music, something soft and vintage.

Diana leant against Zoe's shoulder.

Beatrice curled into a beanbag.

Bethany finally let herself smile.

And I?

I stood quietly in the doorway for a moment, watching them.

Women.

Warriors.

Each of us.

And something in me knew that whatever came next - Vivian's revelation, my past, our tangled histories - we would face it together.

One confession at a time.

One cup of tea at a time.

One glass of wine at a time.

One biscuit at a time.

One get-together at a time.

CHAPTER 25

Secrets Spilled

The next meeting of our Coffee Group was held at Zoe's townhouse. It was the first time we'd gathered there since Zoe had served her husband with the divorce papers. He was gone now, as were the sleek suits, his toothbrush, and the bottle of wine he used to bring to dinner parties as though that excused his infidelities. Zoe was newly alone, but not lonely. There was something in her stance now — shoulders squared, head high — that reminded me of a woman preparing for battle and already knowing she'd win.

We trickled in as usual, bearing contributions of banana bread, gluten-free muffins and overly expensive cheeses we all pretended not to judge. The chatter was easy, light-hearted. Di looked stronger today, though I noticed she was sitting with a cushion behind her back, her eyes ringed with fatigue despite her smile. Beatrice was back to her usual brightness, though she met my eye now and again with a kind of tenderness we hadn't shared before.

Fiona looked more relaxed. Natalie was still showing some concern about the police investigation, but the wine would relax her. Meanwhile, Shanice looked like a whale; she was so big, but her smile said it all. I could swear that George was smelling of bread, and finally Vivian arrived.

She was dressed plainly, in jeans and a pale-blue blouse that brought out the copper tones in her hair. She gave a tight smile as she entered, carrying nothing but her handbag and what I would later come to know was something far heavier.

I felt the moment shift as soon as she walked in. Maybe the others didn't sense it, but I did. I always feel a turn in the air when something is about to change.

We'd just finished pouring the wine when she stood. No one else was speaking, so her voice cut through the hum of the kettle and the soft clink of teaspoons like the start of a storm.

"Eleanor, may I speak to you?"

Every head turned.

Even Fiona put down her biscuit.

I stood. "Of course. Shall we—"

"No," Vivian said gently. "Here. I think it's time."

She reached into her handbag and pulled out an envelope.

Not the usual sort.

It was thick.

Official.

My stomach tightened.

She held it out to me, and I took it, hands already trembling.

"I had a DNA test done," she said.

"I used a sample from one of the old letters I found in the boxes at the historical society — the ones you donated. There was a stamp. I cross-referenced it with my own DNA. I wasn't expecting anything. Not really. But…"

My breath stopped.

She took another envelope out and handed it to Zoe, who was closest. "It's all there. The lab reports. Chain of custody. Everything checked out. I needed to be sure."

I looked down at the envelope in my hand.

I didn't need to open it. I knew what it said.

Vivian's voice dropped to a whisper. "You're my mother, aren't you?"

My knees gave way before my words did.

I sat slowly, as though my body had decided it would bear the truth better than my voice could.

The silence in the room was so complete I could hear the clock ticking in Zoe's kitchen.

I looked at her, at the woman I knew and respected and had secretly grown fond of.

Her eyes were steady.

Not angry.

Just searching.

Searching for something I wasn't sure I had the right to give.

"Yes," I said. "Yes, Vivian. I am."

A sound escaped someone's lips, maybe Shanice's or Bethany's - I could not tell - like the breath of an entire room being let go.

"I wanted to tell you," I continued, my voice shaking. "I've been carrying the guilt for so long. I never thought I would get the chance to say it aloud. Not to you."

"Why didn't you?" she asked.

"Because I was a coward. Because I convinced myself, it would be crueller to reappear in your life and disturb whatever happiness you might have found. And because I didn't believe I deserved to be forgiven."

Vivian looked down. Her shoulders shook once. Then again.

And then she crossed the room slowly, deliberately, and sat beside me. I reached for her hand.

She didn't pull away.

The tears came fast then from both of us.

Not wailing and not grief. Just release.

Around us, the others sat stunned, quiet.

A couple of sniffles here and there.

I saw Zoe's hand cover her mouth, Fiona blinking hard.

Even Beatrice looked like her yoga breathing wasn't working.

Di, of all people, was the first to move.

She stood, came around the table and gently placed a hand on both our shoulders.

"Family is complicated," she said softly. "But it's still family. And what you two just did, owning your truth like that, it's the bravest thing I've seen in years."

Vivian let out a breath that sounded halfway between a laugh and a sob. I wiped my eyes with a napkin someone passed me and looked around the room.

"I spent years writing fiction to protect myself from my story," I said. "And now here we are, living one that's more moving than anything I could've imagined."

The circle of women leant in then — not literally, but emotionally.

Their energy.

Their warmth.

Their presence.

We weren't alone. Not anymore. Not in our pain. Not in our joy.

Beatrice raised her glass. "To truth. However messy and late it arrives."

We clinked mugs and wine glasses and even Zoe's borrowed tumbler of coconut water.

And in that moment, as Vivian and I sat side by side, fingers still intertwined, I felt something settle.

Maybe not healing. Not yet. But this was only the beginning of it.

We were all finally telling our stories.

And maybe, just maybe, that was what would save us.

CHAPTER 26

The Phone Call

Once again, the next gathering was at my place, and the atmosphere crackled with something close to giddy relief.

It was as if the collective weight of secrets — heavy, silent burdens each of us had carried for too long — had finally been tossed into the centre of the room, where they no longer threatened to suffocate us.

We weren't exposed exactly. We were just seen. And oddly, that didn't feel frightening anymore.

Naomi brought over three bottles of sparkling rosé she'd been saving for a "proper occasion".

Apparently, this qualified.

Bethany arrived with two trays of her infamous mini quiches — one with the crust and one gluten-free – which caused a bit of good-natured debate about which version was better. (Verdict: crusted, by a landslide.)

Georgina breezed in last, triumphant and still buzzing from the successful launch of her new store in Picton.

"Oh, please," she said, waving off the compliments but beaming with pride all the same. "You lot didn't give me a tough time; you gave me an excellent time. I needed that. And by the way, Eleanor, you owe me a replacement lavender diffuser.

Someone looking at Bethany knocked mine over during the 'impromptu conga line' situation."

Bethany smirked and raised her glass. "Worth it."

We all laughed loudly and honestly.

And for the first time in what felt like months, maybe years,

I let myself join in fully. No internal editor, no polite restraint.

Later, as the conversation drifted from local gossip to travel dreams and Naomi's newfound obsession with jigsaw puzzles, my phone vibrated on the bench behind me.

I glanced down and froze.

Robert Clarke.

I slipped away to the hallway and pressed Accept.

"Hello?"

"Eleanor, hi. I hope I'm not interrupting anything."

"Not at all." I stepped further away from the dining room, the laughter behind me now muffled. "Is everything okay?"

"I need to see you in person," Robert said. His voice was tight, controlled but barely. "When can we meet?"

"Why in person?" I asked. "Robert, you're worrying me. Can't you just tell me?"

There was a pause.

Then, carefully: "Because you will not believe what I found out. And I need to show it to you."

My heart tapped faster against my ribs.

"The next gathering isn't an option," I said. "It's a private night just for the ladies. Georgina's hosting us at the store."

"I understand," he said. "The week after then?"

"Yes," I said, trying to keep my voice even. "The week after. My place again. Thursday?"

"Thursday works. And Eleanor..."

"Yes?"

"Thank you for looking into my mother. You've started something I didn't know I needed."

We ended the call gently, and I stood in the dim light of the hallway for a few seconds, staring at my reflection in the hall mirror.

Something had shifted. I couldn't explain it, but I felt it.

Like standing on the edge of a cliff, aware that a gust of wind could push you forward into something terrifying or exhilarating.

I rejoined the others just as Zoe was describing the look on her soon-to-be-ex-husband's face when she told him to "take his toothbrush, his tennis trophies, and his girlfriend's dog and get out".

The room erupted again, but I could only smile faintly.

My thoughts had drifted back to Robert, back to Margaret Clarke, back to a past I never expected would circle its way into my present.

Whatever Robert had found, it would change something. I knew it.

And, ready or not, I had one more week to prepare.

CHAPTER 27

The Bakery

The night at Georgina's new bakery in Picton felt like something out of a novel—one of those rare, golden evenings when the air seems lighter, the food richer, and everyone is just a little more generous with their laughter.

We'd pushed three café tables together and draped them with mismatched linen napkins from home, lit tall candles that flickered wildly with the opening and closing of the front door. The scent of cardamom buns and cherry-glazed tarts clung to everything, even our hair. It was warm; it was easy; and, for once, no one was pretending.

So much had changed since we'd first gathered, all stiff smiles and surface pleasantries. Now, the women of the Northport group didn't just bring food—they brought their truths.

Zoe, finally free from the shadow of her husband's deception, had launched headfirst into a consulting gig with a local not-for-profit.

"I figured if I've spent half my life cleaning up messes, I might as well get paid for it."

Her tone was light, but her eyes shone with something deeper.

Purpose.

The group had rallied around her like a Greek chorus with wine, vengeance, and spreadsheets. Naomi had even helped her find the right solicitor.

Naomi herself had come to the last two meetings without makeup, which, for her, was an emotional striptease.

She looked softer.

Realer.

Since confronting Michael and confessing her anonymous support of his family, she said she'd felt like her skin fit differently.

"There's shame, sure," she'd told me the week before, "but there's also relief. I don't have to lie to myself anymore."

Bethany, the ever-glamorous, silver-haired mystery of the group, had been the biggest surprise. After admitting she'd once been involved in a long-ago political heist and her son was in prison (two details we still couldn't quite wrap our heads around), she seemed to grow younger by the week.

Maybe it was the weight that had lifted, or maybe it was the thrill of finally telling someone. Either way, she walked with a little bounce in her kitten heels now, and Georgina had begun calling her "The Dame" with affectionate reverence.

Georgina's own transformation was subtler, but no less significant.

Her store in Picton had become a sanctuary for herself and for us. The front counter always had fresh blooms from the market, and behind it, she wore an apron that read Flour Child.

She still threw sarcastic barbs with frightening precision, but her laughter lasted longer now, and she didn't disappear early like she used to.

As for me, I had stopped pretending I wasn't still haunted by the past.

I leant into it.

I let it speak.

And in return, it gave me the courage to write again. My novel—the one that had been a shapeless fog in my mind—now had a name, a structure, and a first chapter I didn't hate.

And, of course, I regained my daughter Vivian.

The wine flowed as easily as the stories that night.

Second helpings became third.

Naomi brought out a platter of fig and blue cheese tartlets that didn't stand a chance.

At some point, Zoe tried to teach us how to play a card game she claimed was "big in Berlin", but we were too far gone in laughter and wine to get through the rules.

Eventually, as the night wound down, and the candles melted into puddles, we began talking about the next gathering.

"My place?" Bethany offered, adjusting her scarf. "I'll even let you snoop through my bookshelf this time."

Georgina grinned. "Only if you spike the tea like last time. I still swear there was something in that chamomile."

But I shook my head and raised my glass.

"Actually, I was hoping you'd all come back to my place."

There was a brief silence as everyone turned toward me.

I wasn't usually the one to insist. I hosted, yes—but rarely pushed.

"Again?" asked Natalie.

"I've got an extra chair to put out," I added casually.

Zoe's eyes narrowed with playful suspicion. "Oh? Are we expecting a guest?"

Naomi leant in, lips curved in curiosity. "Who is it?"

I gave nothing away.

Just one sentence, smooth and deliberate: "I might have one more secret to share."

The room buzzed with instant speculation.

Georgina nearly dropped her wineglass.

Bethany clutched her pearls with dramatic flair.

"Don't be coy, Eleanor," Georgina said. "We've all spilled our guts. Don't you dare hold out on us?"

But I just smiled and refilled her glass.

"You'll find out soon enough."

Because I did have a secret.

One more thread in the tangled tapestry of our lives that I hadn't dared unravel until now. And if Robert Clarke kept his promise, that last piece might arrive sooner than I expected.

For the first time in years, I wasn't afraid of the truth.

I was ready to set another place at the group.

CHAPTER 28

The Empty Chair

I hadn't realised until Zoe raised her glass and tapped the side with her spoon—spilling a little of the Cabernet, of course—that this was our one-year anniversary. One year of secrets and tears, of hard truths and unexpected friendships. It had been a year since a simple invitation to coffee had become something much more—a lifeline, a confessional, a sanctuary for twelve women with too much history and not enough places to put it.

The mood was lighter tonight, even celebratory.

Jokes ricocheted from one corner of the room to another like a game of verbal ping-pong. Naomi had brought a ridiculous tiara she insisted each of us take turns wearing for a "truth round", and it now perched lopsidedly on Bethany's freshly permed hair as she recounted a scandalous misadventure from her youth involving a Spanish sailor, a locked wine cellar and a mistaken identity.

The food was plentiful—Georgina had outdone herself with platters of baked Brie and lemon shortbread.

Even Shanice, poor thing, overdue by a day and looking like she might pop right there in my lounge, nibbled on some melon and sipped her tea between frequent and increasingly exasperated trips to the bathroom.

"You'd think this baby was training for a marathon with how much I'm running tonight," she groaned, prompting a chorus of sympathetic laughter.

But even as the laughter filled the house, there was something else in the air—an undercurrent of quiet anticipation. Eleven women sat comfortably in the lounge, but it was the twelfth seat that drew their glances.

The empty chair.

The one I'd placed by the fireplace with quiet deliberation earlier that afternoon.

The one that meant something.

At precisely 8:32 p.m., the doorbell rang.

My stomach twisted slightly, though I smiled as I crossed the hallway. I opened the door.

There he stood.

Robert Clinton Clarke.

Crisp button-down, blazer, nervous eyes.

He looked younger than I thought, or perhaps just more vulnerable.

"Evening, Robert," I said gently. "Come in."

He stepped inside, blinking at the unexpected crowd. I guided him toward the lounge, where conversations faded and eyes fixed curiously on the newcomer.

He began awkwardly. "I didn't realise you were having company. I expected just you, Eleanor."

"You said it was something I wouldn't believe," I said calmly, gesturing toward the empty chair.

"And these women are part of the reason I'm standing here today, capable of hearing it. So, if you're willing, Robert—share it with all of us."

There was a brief pause.

Then Robert nodded. "Alright."

He sat.

Cleared his throat.

Looked around the circle of curious, supportive faces.

"My mother, Margaret Clarke, showed up in a photo that Eleanor shared with me. Something she found. The picture also had another person in it. Eleanor's husband."

The room was hushed now. Only the tick of the antique clock over the mantel broke the silence.

"I started digging," he continued. "It wasn't easy. But I traced her movements through charity records, old correspondences. I followed a trail that led me to an old file in a community centre archive—Northport Women's Shelter, 1987."

A few of the women shifted slightly in their seats.

"She'd been hiding. From someone. Or something. I don't know the full extent yet, but there were coded notes in her journal, people she trusted. People who helped her. And one name kept coming up again and again."

He turned to look directly at me.

"Eleanor Whitman."

I froze. The name hit like an echo I didn't know I'd been waiting to hear.

"You knew her," he said softly. "Maybe you don't remember. Or maybe you do, and you've locked it away. But

Margaret wrote about you. About how kind you were. About how you helped her."

My throat was suddenly dry. "I don't know... I do not remember her. Why don't I remember her? It is all a blank, Robert. Tell me what you found out, please."

"You were younger. Before you were Eleanor Whitman. But she never forgot you."

He leant forward now, voice lowered but urgent.

"Margaret was in trouble. And you're the only one who helped her."

A collective breath seemed to be held across the room.

"What kind of trouble?" Naomi asked, ever the practical one.

"Is she alive?" Zoe whispered.

"Where is she now?" Georgina pressed.

But Robert didn't answer.

He looked back at me with something between fear and hope.

"I need to show you something," he said. "All of you."

He reached into his satchel and unzipped it slowly.

And just as he drew out a folded map, yellowed with age and covered in strange handwritten symbols, there was a loud, urgent knock on the front door.

We all turned.

Another visitor?

Before I could move, the knock came again.

This time louder.

Robert's hand stopped mid-motion. His eyes darted to mine.

"Eleanor," he said, barely a whisper, "I think we've run out of time."

I stood frozen, heart hammering in my chest, then the doorbell rang again.

And the lights flickered.

I went to the door. Robert standing behind me, opened it and froze......

About the Author

José F. Nodar

Flung into one of life's biggest challenges at just eleven, José's story began in Havana, Cuba. The Cuban Revolution forced him onto a plane alone, landing him at an orphanage in a small Georgia town called Washington. Reuniting with his parents wouldn't happen until he was eighteen, a high school graduate in Atlanta.

Business Administration became his focus at Georgia State University. From there, he navigated the world of finance, first at the First National Bank of Atlanta (now Wells Fargo) and later as a project manager in financial consulting. These roles took him across the United States, Europe, and even Australia.

It was in Camden, New South Wales, Australia, that a spark ignited José's creative side. A writers' group became the launching pad for his debut novel, and soon, his mind birthed Danny Monk, his first major character.

But José's life isn't all about writing. When he's not crafting captivating stories, you might find him at the local mall, observing the world and gathering inspiration for future characters. Away from his computer, he dives into books or enjoys long strolls around Spring Farm.

Publication Year for Books by José F. Nodar

Published in 2022

Books, Pens & Larceny

Stories to Share with My Partner Book 1

Stories to Share with My Partner Book 2

Stories to Share with My Partner Book 3

Published in 2023

Stories to Share with My Partner Book 4

Published in 2024

Libros, Bolígrafos y Hurto

El Autobús del Tiempo

Cuentos Para Compartir con Mi Pareja Libro 1

Cuentos Para Compartir con Mi Pareja Libro 2

Cuentos Para Compartir con Mi Pareja Libro 3

Stories to Share with My Partner Book 5

Quick Stories & Poem Volume I

Quick Stories & Poem Volume II

Mending Hearts at Crystal Cove

The Universe Between Us

The Time Bus

SEX

Published in 2025

Stories to Share with My Partner Book 6

Stories to Share with My Partner Book 7

Stories to Share with My Partner Book 8

Stories to Share with My Partner Book 9

The KDP Blueprint

A Love Finally Spoken

The Ghost Detective's First Case

The Compass Legacy

A Night of Love

Quick Stories & Poem Volume III

The Hamster Who Whispered Back

The Teacher's Assistant

Reparando Corazones en Crystal Cove

Published in 2026

Stories to Share with My Partner Book 10

Stories to Share with My Partner Book 12

Stories to Share with My Partner Book 13

Stories to Share with My Partner Book 14

Stories to Share with My Partner Book 16

Stories to Share with My Partner Book 17

Stories to Share with My Partner Book 18

Stories to Share with My Partner Book 1

Stories to Share with My Partner Book 20

Whispers from My Wife

Maybe This Is Everything

Locker 217

Love in Stereo

Somewhere in Time

The Northport Coffee Group

The Last Light of Aurethis

The Clause That Killed Him

Somewhere in Time

Between Sessions

The Girl That Didn't Come Home

The Ones that Got Way

The Ghosts We Owe

Una Noche de Amor

Un Amor Finalmente Declarado